CLAIMING HIS NEED

FERAL BREED MOTORCYCLE CLUB
BOOK TWO

D1563852

ELLIS LEIGH

Claiming His Need
Copyright ©2014 by Ellis Leigh
All rights reserved
ISBN: 978-0-9862371-1-9

Kinship Press
P.O. Box 221
Prospect heights, IL 60070

Dedicated to Caren, for never giving up, always tracking me down when I disappear into my writing cave for too long, and being a touchstone when I need one. You inspire me to write better, write hotter, and make it more sultry.

Thank you for always being there.

ONE

MAGNUS WAS ABOUT TO get his dick bit off.

Truthfully, that's probably what he deserved for sticking that thing down the throat of whatever woman would let him fuck her mouth. The woman he'd chosen this time, though, didn't seem all that thrilled with the aggressive way he was handling her.

Even after walking the earth for almost four hundred years, it still surprised me what people would do for money.

"Hmmm, fuck. Yeah, that's it. Take it all, you filthy cunny."

I held back a growl and slouched in my chair. Magnus set the tone and made the rules for our motorcycle club of wolf shifters. He may have been only the vice president of the den, but with our president, Rebel, on sabbatical with his new mate, Magnus stood as the highest-ranking officer in the club.

As his Sergeant-at-Arms, I helped ensure the rules were followed. One rule Magnus had set was to open the lower Detroit denhouse to the local prostitutes. He called it "supporting local business"; I called it putting the entire Detroit crew of the Great Lakes den at risk of exposure. And one risk the Feral Breed fought against was exposing wolf shifters to the human population.

But Magnus needed his dick sucked, and so the women were allowed inside the old warehouse on the city's southwest side. The neighborhood a shithole, but Magnus favored it due to the lack of law enforcement. Not that the city had a huge police presence, but the southwest side was particularly industrial and therefore deserted in the evenings. Fewer homes meant fewer witnesses, which meant the two forms of business most prevalent in the area after dark were drug deals and prostitution. I much preferred the denhouse on the border of Grosse Pointe—the one where I kept an apartment on the second floor. But we spent an inordinate amount of time in this piece of shit building in a neighborhood that reeked of rendered animal fat and sulfur fumes because of Magnus. And his need to get his dick sucked.

Rebel needed to get his ass on his bike and his head in the game before I took a chunk out of Magnus' hide.

"Ung, yeah... A little more. Take it...take all of it, girl. Oh, yeah."

The sound of wood scraping across concrete meant one of my Breed brothers had decided to enter this particular level of hell. The poor sap. At a muffled chuckle, I whipped my head up from where I'd been staring at the filthy floor beneath my feet. Sandman spun the chair opposite and straddled it, setting his beer on the table as he did.

"Someday that asshole is going to find his mate, and I truly hope she's the biggest ball-busting shewolf ever bred. He and Scab both deserve a little emasculation."

I snorted even as the sounds coming from the alcove behind me made me want to gag. "I believe that would be called karma."

Sandman's face grew serious. "You could get up and walk away, you know."

"It's my job to be here." I cringed as Magnus groaned in the background. "I'm supposed to protect the den, remember?"

"You're a stronger man than I, Gatekeeper." He tipped his beer toward me before bringing the amber glass to his lips.

"I'm here because that filthy fuck likes to get off with human women who can never know who we truly are. One slip and the entire den goes down." I narrowed my eyes. "What's your excuse?"

Sandman grinned. "Numbers has a pool going to see how long the young buck lasts. It's on some kind of sliding-scale progressive thing that I'm nowhere near smart enough to understand. The guys sent me over here to help pinpoint the exact moment of splooge."

I glanced at the group of shifters across the room. They all avoided eye contact, preferring to look at the walls or the floor as I surveyed them. Two stood with their backs to me, their leather vests sporting only a Great Lakes rocker, no growling wolf patch or Feral Breed rocker.

"Pup One and Pup Two are in on the bet?"

"They think they are. Club rules will be honored, though— if a prospect gambles and wins, the money goes to the house."

I shook my head and chuckled. "I'd hate to be standing next to you when karma catches up with *your* ass."

"I didn't make the rules; I'm only playing by them." Sandman frowned and looked down at the table. "Besides, I'm pretty sure karma's taken more than her fill from me."

I grunted my agreement and tried to tune out the filth falling from Magnus' lips. Tried and failed.

"Fuck...you gonna take it? Swallow me down? Yeah, that's it. I like a little teeth. Yeah."

I placed my elbows on the table and my head in my hands as I waited for him to blow his load. No man should have to hear how another man likes to get his rocks off. There's something seriously fucked up about knowing what he was going to say and how close he was to coming based on the language he used.

"That's it, that's it. Yeah. Hot...so hot. Gonna come so hard. Swallow it, girl. Swallow me down."

Finally. I glanced at my phone. Eight minutes had passed since he'd dragged the poor girl past the guys with a smirk on his face. An eight-minute blow job from a halfway decent trick meant the boss probably wouldn't bitch too much for the next three days. Overall, I figured it was almost worth listening to him spout off about how hot and wet her mouth was in exchange for those few days of peace. As my denmates and I had learned quickly, when Magnus wasn't happy, we all paid the price.

A groan, a few whispered words, and the shuffle of fabric sliding into place told me my time in hell was almost over. I clenched my teeth and locked my wolf instincts down tight. I knew what was coming even before I heard the offer. It was the same every time. Magnus would die his little death and then...

"You up for it, Gates? She's got a hot mouth just waiting for your junk."

I glanced over my shoulder at the younger man and then to the woman still on her knees. No, not woman. Or if so, just barely. She looked like a child to me, too young to be dealing with men like Magnus for a little coin.

Making my point for me, Magnus grabbed her by the back of the hair and tugged, pulling her head back so her mouth fell open.

"It's a pretty mouth. All wet and swollen from letting me fuck it. Didn't even mind when I pulled her hair. Did you, sweetheart?"

The girl stared up at him but said nothing. Funny, who would've thought we'd have so much in common? I wasn't going to say anything either.

I hated when Magnus acted like some kind of badass, hated his disrespectful attitude toward women. It was against our modern culture, against the very fabric of a society of creatures who mated for life, and I was sick of bearing witness to it. Not that a handful of the traditional packs didn't still do things most of the rest of the species found reprehensible. Calling an Alpha Prerogative, forced shewolf breedings, violence toward the unmated males of the pack—our species as a whole had not always behaved in ways that would make me proud. But the tide had turned over a century ago after an uprising among one of the largest traditional packs in the country. Sandman's former pack.

"So what do you think, Sergeant? You want in on this?"

Every inch of me burned and my muscles ached with the need to shift. The disrespect Magnus showed by calling me by my position instead of my road name made me want to beat the fucker into the ground. I was not "Sergeant." I was Gatekeeper, feared executioner of the Feral Breed, brother to the Beast, and protector of the shifters in my territory. My denmates called me Gates. The men I hunted called me their biggest fear. The little fucker did not get to call me "Sergeant."

I twisted in my seat and placed my elbow on the back of the chair, never taking my eyes off the younger, weaker shifter. I kept my chin tilted so the girl couldn't see my face, and then I called forth my wolf spirit. I didn't need a mirror to know what Magnus would see. The way my eyes would seem to glow with the power of the animal biding his time inside of me, how the black fur of my wolf form would begin to fill in like a mask across my face, a peek of the tips of my canines as they extended past my lips.

"No, thank you, sir."

Magnus froze for a moment, eyes wide and jaw tight. It would have been comical had this not been the man who'd been assigned to lead us. He was no leader.

Shaking off his instincts, Magnus forced himself to relax, releasing the natural fear a full challenge from a stronger wolf shifter released. The stupid fuck. He thought I didn't have the balls to throw a challenge at him. Truth was, I simply didn't care anymore. I'd been walking the earth for over four centuries, had watched better shifters than he rise and fall as the power within our breed ebbed and swelled, and I'd killed a lot more men than any other Feral Breed member. Magnus was as significant in my life as a single thorn on a rosebush. One little prick among thousands.

"You don't know what you're missing, Gates."

I gave Magnus a toothy grin as I imagined all the ways I could eviscerate him in my human form. It'd be quicker if I partial-shifted. Perhaps just a paw. Or the tip of a paw. A single claw would do the trick.

An arrogant chuckle and a pat to the poor girl's head and Magnus was striding past me, shades in place and leather cut on his back. I hated seeing him with a fully-patched vest. He didn't deserve to be a patched member. He hadn't earned those colors, in my opinion. But Blaze had thought otherwise, and as national president of the club, he outranked us all. Magnus was the one officer in all of the Feral Breed Motorcycle Club who was not voted in by his denmates, which made him the most ineffectual leader in the country. And with Rebel gone, we were stuck with him.

As soon as Magnus disappeared into the crowd of Breed members by the bar, the girl stood on shaky legs and pushed her hair off her face. "Can I interest either of you gentlemen in a date?"

"No." The word came out on a growl. Sandman shot me a hard look. I shrugged. I wasn't interested in anything she had to offer, and I didn't want her in the denhouse.

"No, thank you, hon. Why don't you head on home?" Sandman stood and led her to the door while whispering in her ear. He shook her hand before she left, which I found odd. When he turned and met my scrutiny, I tilted my head and waited for him to answer my unspoken question.

"I gave her some cash to get home."

I huffed. "This isn't Chicago. That cash isn't going to help her get home because there're no fucking cabs. She'll be lucky if she's able to find a bus running anywhere near where she needs to go. Besides, she's probably from this neighborhood."

"I had to do something." He looked away, avoiding my eyes. "She reminded me of my Margaret."

I swallowed hard and ran a hand over my face. Sandman invoking the name of Margaret let him get away with things no other shifter could. But the story of the death of Sandman's mate was legendary among the Feral Breed; hell, it was a legend told in warning to traditional packs.

My cell phone vibrating across the table made the memories of darker times evaporate. I grabbed the device and stepped away from the table for privacy.

"Gates here."

"It's Half Trac."

I squeezed my eyes closed. A call from Blaze's vice president always meant the same thing. We were needed. And while normally the idea of a new mission would give me an adrenaline rush, those few words from Half Trac, along with the memories of how we'd come to have Sandman in our den, did nothing but make me feel every long year I'd been alive.

Not wanting to keep Half Trac waiting, I spun and glanced around the room. Finally, my eyes landed on my road captain, a shifter by the name of Klutch. He caught my gaze quickly and hurried over as I turned my attention back to the phone.

"Good evening, sir. What's the situation?"

"I need a team to ride as soon as possible. Alpha Wariksen of the Valkoisus pack called regarding a possible territory dispute. Many of his pack are leaving for a fishing run, so he's asking for backup should things go sour."

"Any particular reason he believes he needs backup?"

Half Trac paused, telling me more than any words could. "He didn't say, but I got the feeling there was something he was withholding about the need for protection. I would recommend you go with a full team to be on the safe side."

"Five riders heading to the Upper Peninsula." I glanced at Klutch, who nodded and pointed to his watch. "How soon should we be there?"

"Wariksen wants protection as soon as possible."

"Of course he does." I mouthed *now* to Klutch. He spun and hurried toward the rest of the crew to assign the team. "It's a nine-hour drive from here. Let the Alpha know we'll be there first thing in the morning."

Half Trac chuckled. "It's always such a pleasure doing business with you, Gatekeeper."

"That's good to hear, sir."

The powerful shifter was still chuckling when I pressed end and walked toward my brothers.

"Half Trac says we roll, and we need five." I nodded at Klutch. "So, who's on the team?"

Klutch pointed to the front row of shifters. "You, Shadow, Sandman, Magnus, and Pup One. You could pull Numbers in over the prospect if you'd like or if you think you'll need the war wagon."

I glanced between the two shifters in question. I liked them both; they were strong, smart, and easy to work with. But Pup One had nearly died in Milwaukee when Rebel met his mate, and he hadn't been on a mission since. He needed to get back on the horse, so to speak. A simple territory dispute would be the perfect back-to-work project for him.

"I'll keep Pup. Numbers can hang back on this one." I turned to head for the rear of the warehouse where we used what was once a manufacturing space to store our bikes. No way were we parking our girls on the street.

"Sandman, you'll be captaining this trip since Klutch isn't joining us," Magnus yelled. "Let's load up and move out. It's a long fucking drive, and we've got a limited number of hours to make it in."

I swung open the door to the garage and nearly grinned at the sight. Hundreds of motorcycles filled the space. Just about any make, model, and color one could think of—from stock bikes to custom choppers, crotch-rockets to baggers. Every possible option waited for us to take it out for a spin, though there was only one bike I wanted. My favorite…my baby.

I strode straight to my classic Indian Chief Blackhawk and threw my leg over her. While all the other guys chose their newest models for this trek, I wanted my old girl for reasons I couldn't explain. She just felt like the right piece of steel to have with me. Everything about the bike had been customized over the years. The chrome exhaust, the chumps handlebars, the leather bitch-seat add-on—the bike was one-hundred-percent mine.

"Think you can keep up on that thing, old man?"

Sandman straddled a Ducati crotch-rocket a few spots over. His bike definitely had the horsepower we needed, as well as a style that screamed badass. But it lacked the finesse of my favorite lady. Where his bike looked like speed and aggression, mine looked like a classic pinup beauty. A beauty that could tear past any bike in the warehouse without even coming close to the red line.

"You worry about your own self, young one. My girl and I will do just fine."

Sandman grinned and started his engine. The deep whine echoed off the metal walls. Three others soon joined in the noise, the whole building beginning to shake with the vibrations.

With a glance at Sandman and a nod to Magnus, I kick-started my engine, the throaty rumble of American ingenuity louder than anything else in the warehouse. The leather seat gave with my weight as I pushed off into a slow roll. We followed Magnus out of the building, falling into our road order as we headed north. Soon, the white concrete of the highway was flying by under our tires. We had nine hours to make it to a rough, secluded section of the Keweenaw Peninsula. It was going to be a long, hard ride.

TWO

Kaija

MOTHER NATURE HATED ME. An unquenchable thirst was ravaging my body. My skin itched with a burn I couldn't soothe, my joints popped like hot grease in a pan, and my blood scalded my veins as it ran through my body. Every inch of me ached with my upcoming heat cycle, but I refused to let it show. Not that most of my packmates wouldn't know; I was sure they could all smell the hormone cocktail my body threw off as I burned alive from the inside out. I just hoped the majority would be respectful enough to keep the knowledge to themselves.

"I can't believe you've called in those animals. They're hardly better than the nomads trying to push us out of our territory. " Elder Donati stood in the center of the great room, his face red with what could only be described as rage. He and my father had been arguing for hours over the obvious signs of a nomad invasion onto Valkoisus Pack land.

"They have come before to aid us when we needed them. I remember no issues with their respect of pack law, Elder." My father stood in front of the fireplace with his arms crossed. He loomed over the smaller Donati clan leader, his Alpha rank obvious in body language as well as mass.

"Then perhaps you should learn from them, Alpha Wariksen. Your own respect of pack law seems to be lacking in regards to your family."

My father's face grew hard as he clenched his jaw. Soon, the vein in his forehead would begin to throb. He would roar and growl and order the other shifters to bend to his will. Whether they liked it or not, he was Alpha of the pack, a strong leader, and a stronger opponent. There was no one I knew of who could possibly best him. And yet the Donati clan consistently pushed and tested their boundaries like errant teenagers.

Bored with the back-and-forth, I left the men to their argument on the other side of the room and turned my attention to my youngest nephews. The two sat beside each other on the fabric of the scarlet Alpha family cloak I wore, their own little cloaks wrapped around their chubby legs.

"No no, Luka. We don't eat our brother's shoes." I wagged my finger at the toddler and replaced the now-sodden shoe with a nubby teether ring. "Here you go, baby."

"You're good with them."

I glanced at Lanie, my newest packsister, as she settled herself on the couch behind me. I envied her the ability to wear jeans and sweaters whenever she wanted to. While the cloaks were comfortable and perfect for shifters who tended to destroy regular clothes on a daily basis, they were old-fashioned and not particularly flattering. I much preferred the human clothes I'd begun to wear when I was alone in my suite.

"I love these two rascals. They're like mini-versions of my brother."

"Which one? You have a few, you know."

I rolled my eyes. "Dante, of course. His sons are tiny carbon copies of him."

"Now, there's a scary thought. Two more Dantes terrorizing

this place? The entire Donati clan would secede from the pack."

"Good riddance," I whispered. Lanie raised an eyebrow, but I ignored it and smiled at my adorable nephews instead. I hadn't been kidding when I'd said they were like mini-Dantes. They looked exactly like him when he was a young boy, the shifter genes overriding the human ones. Where Dante's mate, Collette, was tall with dark skin, raven hair, and brown eyes, the boys were fair and blond like the rest of the Wariksen shifters. They even had our dimples.

My other three nephews, the triplets, were a mix of their parents. Bernte had mated another shifter, so the darker hair and eyes that two of the boys had were more to be expected. Only one looked like a Wariksen. I couldn't wait for Lanie and my twin brother Rex to have babies. They'd been mated only a few months, so I expected a bit of a delay. Though with mating season coming, and lots of cold months to hunker down against the frigid Upper Peninsula air, they might surprise us with a summer baby. I truly hoped for it. With five nephews and no nieces, I had a strong yearning for all things pink and frilly.

"What are they arguing about now?" Lanie asked when the voices grew louder. As a human mate, she was not always present at these meetings. But with Dante away on a fishing trip for our business, Collette and the boys were spending a lot of time at the Alpha house. Unfortunately, Collette had come down with a cold, so Lanie had been hanging around to help me with the boys. Trying to corral two shifter pups under the age of two could drive anyone to madness. Mother Nature must have laughed at us all as she blessed us with twins, triplets, and more. Single births were simply unheard of in the Wariksen family.

I snuck a peek at the group of men and women on the other side of the great room. Representatives from each family clan of the Valkoisus Pack were present, as well as the Alpha male and female. My oldest brother, Bernte—Dante's twin—stood in as leader of the Wariksen clan, his dark maroon cloak declaring his Alpha family status. My father, as Alpha, could not vote on his own family's behalf.

"The nomads have come onto pack land again." I turned back to my packsister. "Not fully into camp, but far enough that the Helina clan will be staying at the Alpha house until the boat returns tomorrow. Their cabins are too far out to monitor without straining the guards. Father called the NALB to request assistance from the Feral Breed, and Elder Donati isn't happy about it."

Lanie cocked her head and frowned, her coffee-colored hair falling in waves along her shoulders. She glanced at the pack leaders and then leaned forward to make sure no one else would hear her. "I know the NALB is the Lycan Brotherhood leadership, right? They make the rules for the packs. I don't think I've ever heard of the Feral Breed."

"You're sort of correct. Many of the laws of our kind are pack-specific. The NALB oversees the basic covenants of all shifters, like keeping the secret and which groups are allotted land. The Feral Breed is kind of like their mercenary team. They help enforce the rules the NALB dictate."

"So why is it a bad thing your father called them?"

"It's not." I shook my head and shot a quick glance at my father. "Donati's just fired up about something and is using the Breed as his excuse to fight."

"Oh." Lanie sat back, pulling young Eli into her lap as she did. "So what's got his panties in a twist?"

I smiled at the silly phrase. The way she spoke was so different than most of the pack. Of course, most of the pack was ten times as old as the young human.

"I'm not sure, though I think it has something to do with me."

"Why would you think that?"

"They keep looking at me. And"—I glanced around to be sure no one could overhear—"I'm about to go into heat."

Lanie's eyes opened wide, and she leaned forward to keep the conversation as private as possible. "I thought shewolves only went into heat in the winter."

I shrugged, feigning nonchalance even as her words added weight to the lead ball in my stomach. "We do."

"Well…damn. You're early."

"Exactly."

"Have you talked to your father about that huge coming-out thing you wolfy-types have? Where you invite all the other wolfy-types to come sniff you or whatever."

I snorted a laugh. "The Gathering. It's not a chance for shifters to sniff me, but to meet me in the hopes that one of the male shifters will be my mate. It's a huge event held every year, very formal with rules and guidelines to avoid the possibility of interpack fighting. It's also one huge party for the entire Lycan Brotherhood. I want to go to one so badly, but Father hasn't mentioned if we will attend this year. He refused me when I asked last year. He said it wouldn't be safe for me because of the whole Omega thing. I guess I wasn't ready."

"Well, I'm pretty sure you're ready now."

"One can only hope." I swallowed hard as a flare up sent my temperature rocketing. Unmated and quickly coming into my first heat… Mother Nature didn't just hate me; she wanted to see me suffer.

"Aunt Kai," Luka said. He had a peculiar look upon his face as he danced from foot to foot.

"I know that move, buddy." I stood and grabbed his hand. "Do you need to use the potty too, Eli?"

"Potty!" The little imp jumped off Lanie's lap and hurried ahead of me toward the bathroom off the rear hallway.

"Need any help?" Lanie asked.

"No, you relax. I can handle them both for a few minutes."

"Good luck." She smirked as she settled into the corner of the couch. She glanced around the room with an anxious expression before seeming to shrink. I needed to hurry the boys along. I hated to see her look so alone and small. If Rex wasn't busy preparing his crew to leave for the next week-long fishing trip of Wariksen Whitefish, he'd be sitting right beside her. My twin's mate was far too shy to hold her own in a room full of old shifters. She'd disappear into that couch if I let her.

Once the boys were finished in the bathroom, I put Luka on my hip and let Eli run ahead of me through the darkened halls. My family had lived in the Alpha house for as long as I could remember, though it had not always been the case. I knew someday a wolf would challenge my father for position, and then we would be forced to move. I hoped one of my brothers would take over, as my father had become Alpha after besting his own father. Out of all the clans of our pack, we were the most progressive. From what I understood of other packs, not all shifters had the freedoms we did. I couldn't imagine living in a pack with some of the more traditional laws in place. The thought sickened me.

I was halfway between the bathroom and the great room when Chinoo, a younger shifter from the Donati clan, turned the corner and blocked my way.

"Well, don't you look like Little Red Riding Hood in your cloak." He leered at me and approached slowly.

Chinoo and I had never gotten along. When we were little, he would pick on my twin. At the time, Rex was smaller than Chinoo. As soon as Rex began to tower over the irritating shifter, Chinoo tried to become friends with us. Both Rex and I saw right through him, though. As we grew up, Chinoo's attention transferred to me. Apparently, my blond hair, blue eyes, and soft curves made him lustful and stupid. He wanted to bed me, and I wanted him to take a giant leap off the nearest cliff.

"Good evening, Chinoo." I nodded and moved as if to walk around him, but he stepped in my path.

"It's fortuitous we meet at this moment, Kaija. I was coming to find you."

I ground my teeth and fought the urge to roll my eyes. "Why would you be looking for me?"

He wrapped a lock of my hair around his finger, spinning the nearly white strands until I was forced to cock my head to keep him from pulling on it.

"I just thought you would want to know who you'll be bedded with this winter."

Angered by his audacity, I snapped my teeth at his hand. I stepped back as Chinoo stumbled, making him release my hair.

"You need to give up this little obsession of yours. I'm not interested in being your bedmate."

He shrugged, a sneer spreading across his face. "Maybe not, but you're an Omega of this pack. Laws state when an unmated Omega comes of age, any male pack member can petition the Alpha to breed her." He stepped closer, crowding me. I clung to Luka as Eli cowered behind my cloak.

"I can smell it, you know. You'll be in your first heat soon, far too early for breeding season. Every male in this pack can smell it on you. They grow hard whenever you walk by. But that secret you've been keeping between your legs will be mine. I'll be the wolf who gets to have you in my bed for months, bedding you whenever I choose under the guise of trying for pups. Too bad your heat came early this year; it'll be all for naught. Well, at least on the pup side. I'll still get exactly what I want."

I raised my chin. "This is not that kind of pack, you cretin. The Omega has to agree to the breed petitions, and I definitely do not. I will not be bred until I have found my mate."

He snorted. "We both know you're not a virgin. Just give it up to me, and I'll think about dropping the breed petition."

I glared at him, fighting the urge to shift and challenge the arrogant man as a way to establish pack order. "I wouldn't lay with you if you were the last shifter on earth. Your petition is worthless, and so are you."

I stepped around him, but he grabbed my arm and yanked me back. Luka screamed as he nearly fell out of my grasp. Eli, ready and willing to fight any foe who upset his brother, jumped at Chinoo with his teeth bared, a tiny growl rumbling from between his lips.

And then he bit down on Chinoo's calf.

"Fuck. Let go, you little brat." Chinoo jerked his leg, knocking Eli to the ground.

"What's going on here?" Rex came racing down the hall from the front of the house, his maroon cloak swirling behind him.

"This brat bit me." Chinoo pointed at Eli, who was still crying on the ground.

I pulled Luka tighter against me and bent to pick up his brother. "Chinoo here thought it would be a good idea to grab me while I was holding Luka, and it scared him. Eli was just defending his brother."

Rex glared at Chinoo, the power of his wolf an almost physical entity in the small space. "You dared to lay hands on the Alpha's only daughter? The Omega of this pack?"

Chinoo glanced at me, his face growing pale. "I was just informing her of my petition to breed her during the upcoming season."

Rex's eyes met mine and his nostrils flared. My cheeks burned at the realization that he knew how close to my heat cycle I was. But for the first time, I was thankful my family and packmates would know without my telling them. My brothers would never allow a forced breeding.

"Kaija is not expected to breed this season." Rex gave me a wink before returning his attention to Chinoo. "Father's decided she's come of age for a proper mating. He'll be taking her to the annual Gathering in October."

Chinoo positively seethed. "But by shifter law, any male—"

"By pack law," Rex interrupted, "Kaija can choose whether or not to accept a male petitioner into her bed. Do you choose to breed with this wolf, sister?"

"Hell no."

"Fine. That's settled. Now, let's get these boys back where they belong. Plus, I want to find my mate. It's been too long since I've laid eyes on her."

Rex put his hand on my back and escorted me past a furious Chinoo.

"You okay?" he asked once we were out of earshot.

"Of course. Though your lie got my hopes up, and now I'm wishing for things that cannot be."

"What lie?"

"The one about Father taking me to the Gathering this year."

Rex pulled me closer. "It was not a lie, sister-mine. We shall be calling all the packs of the North American Lycan Brotherhood this week to announce your status change. The gods be willing, you will have a mate before the end of the year."

I AWOKE SUDDENLY, THE disorientation of going from sound asleep to wide-awake in a moment making my heart race. I'd been dreaming of my mystery mate—a handsome man with dark hair and bright eyes—laying me down on my bed and doing all sorts of naughty things to me. The dream had been so strong, the face almost clear, and yet something had pulled me out of my bliss and dropped me into the agony of being burned alive with desire.

A scratch at my balcony door had me jolting up in bed. My heart thumped as I looked around my room, clutching my sheet to my naked chest. The curtains floated in the breeze, throwing shadows across the walls and ceiling. I sniffed, trying to catch the scent of another wolf on the breeze, but the perfume of the lavender planted in the flower boxes outside was too strong to grasp anything else.

A second scratching sound set me in motion. I crept out of bed and tiptoed to my hope chest where I'd laid my yoga pants and tank top earlier in the night. I slipped the clothes on and crept along the perimeter of the room. If someone was out on the balcony, I wanted the glass side of the patio door between me and them, not the screen. I'd never thought twice about sleeping with the door open, something I regretted as every tension-filled second ticked by.

Sidling up to the patio door, I leaned my shoulder against the wall and slowly pulled on the linen drapes obscuring my view.

And met a glowing pair of amber eyes in the darkness, looking right at me.

I'd barely yelped when a man burst through the screen, another coming in from the sitting room. The one who'd been outside tackled me to the floor and clamped his hand over my mouth. I bucked and screamed but to no avail; he had me pinned and silenced.

"C'mon, pretty one. You don't want to fight me. Boss man may want you alive, but he didn't say in what condition we needed to deliver you."

I squirmed, but the man, a wolf shifter by the smell of

him, pushed his weight into me, pressing me into the floor. I stiffened, fighting back the burn of a full panic when he ran his nose along my neck and up the underside of my jaw.

"What's this, now? The little bitch is coming into heat? Oh, this is rich. My boys aren't going to be too happy if I don't at least let them get a taste of you, sweetheart."

My stomach knotted in fear as I struggled beneath him once more. When I felt the hard ridge of his erection pressed against my bottom, I kicked and spun, finally knocking the man off my back. With a twist, I stood and readied myself to jump from the balcony. But another shifter rushed through the door from the sitting room before I could make my move, and he wasn't alone.

Lanie, bleeding and unconscious, lay over his shoulder.

"You run and she dies."

I froze. There was no way I could leave my human packsister to these animals. Rex had been alone for so long and had nearly died in his quest to find her. He deserved his happiness. Knowing I needed to buck up and protect the woman I saw as a sister, I pulled myself to my full height and glared at the man who held her captive.

"You hurt her, and you'll have every member of this pack hunting you to hell and back."

He sneered and leaned toward me. "Then I suggest you come along nicely. Boss only wants you. This one is just a bargaining chip if we can't get out of town fast enough."

Biting my lip to keep it from quivering, I nodded my acceptance. Hopefully, the rest of the pack would soon know there was trouble and would come running. I had to keep Lanie alive until then.

The man who'd been on my balcony grabbed my arm and yanked me across the room. "It's time to go, blondie. I expect you to behave, or I'll make sure the human never makes it home alive. And if you even think of going wolf on me, I'll cut your little human pet open and leave her for the animals."

He picked me up and carried me over the patio door threshold onto the balcony. Without pause, he jumped over the stone railing, landing lightly on his feet. Another shifter waited in the shadows of the pine trees surrounding the house.

"Deek caught a shewolf in the woods. I told him he could take her with us. Figured we could relieve a little tension with her and keep the guys' attention off the princess." His eyes raked over my body, and I shivered in response. What I wouldn't give for the loose-fitting, unflattering pack cloak.

"She smells like she's in heat."

"Back off." The shifter holding me growled and gripped me tighter. "Boss wants this one. Let the boys play with the bitch you caught—the Omega is off-limits."

I barely caught the other shifter's nod before the man holding me was running through the woods. Carrying me off to parts unknown while another shifter carried my fragile human sister behind us.

THREE

Gates

JUST INTO WHAT WAS once called Copper Island, we pulled onto Valkoisus Pack land. I immediately knew something was wrong. Men loped through the woods toward what was obviously the Alpha's house, all of them wearing traditional shifter cloaks. That wasn't unusual, though. Many packs wore the cloaks as a way to clothe themselves while still being able to shift on the fly. What didn't seem right was the fact that there were no women to be seen and no children running about.

Because female shifters were a rarity in our breed, many wolves ended up mated to human women. Once their shifter mate marked the human, their aging would slow considerably. Shifters and human mates had been known to live for centuries together, adding children to the family every few years until they chose to stop breeding. This particular pack, being well established, should have had women and pups all over the place. And yet, only men moved outside.

We pulled up to the front porch of the house with Magnus in the lead. The pack shifters watched warily from around the property, guns at the ready. This was not the first time we'd been surrounded by men with firearms. It'd never bothered me too much as the shooter would have to be an excellent shot to do any real damage. But just rolling onto pack land had me on edge. Whether it was being watched by so many shifters or the unfamiliar scent on the air that I couldn't identify, something was making the protective urges in me flare.

"I hate when they wear the cloaks," Sandman said as he glanced at the dark-robed shifters surrounding us. "It's fucking creepy."

Sandman let his bike settle into a lean. He looked one smartass comment away from exploding into a ball of rage. Or fear. Not that I could blame him on either count. Being part of a pack much like this one had lost him his mate.

I met the gaze of one of the pack shifters, a younger man standing on the other side of the driveway. He glared at me, as if I'd personally affronted him somehow by simply riding onto the land. I knew packs had varied opinions about the Breed—from glowing accounts of how we helped them solve a problem, to the whispers and rumors spread about how we were nothing more than nomads with NALB permission to commit crimes against the species. That particular man must have believed the latter.

I held his eyes for nearly a minute, waiting for him to back down, before tiring of his game. He was a pack wolf, probably popular among the traditional set and good at fighting his packmates. But that shit didn't always translate into real world situations. He was a big wolf in a little forest, and I was too far above his level of experience to think about picking a fight. He'd be dead before he took his first breath.

Wanting an end to the stare-off, I called my wolf forward. Not enough to fully shift, but enough to bring about a bit of shape change to my eyes. I waited until I could feel the slight itch of fur filling in along my nose before removing my sunglasses. It took a couple of seconds for the kid to realize what he was seeing as partial shifting was not a skill the majority of pack wolves could master. I knew the moment he figured out why my eyes were encircled in black as he balked and turned away. He must not have been comfortable around bigger, stronger wolves who could partial-shift without effort. Pity, that.

"Quit playing dominance games, would ya?" Magnus spat and rolled his shoulders.

I smirked as we watched the boy scurry around the back of the house.

"He started it."

Sandman snorted. "For someone over four hundred years old, I would have expected a more mature answer."

"Not today, my friend." I swung my leg over the seat of my Indian and strode onto the porch with Sandman and Shadow following right behind me.

"You sure you can keep your cool, Sandy?" Magnus hollered from where he stood beside his bike. "Wouldn't want you to challenge another pack Alpha and cause a riot like last time."

Sandman's head whipped around, his eyes nearly glowing in rage. A growl thundered from deep within him, setting birds to flight and causing every shifter within earshot to freeze in anticipation.

Magnus smirked and crossed his legs at the ankles as he leaned back against the seat of his bagger. "Hey man, I'm just checking. If you're going to be under my watch, you can't be fucking with the rules."

Sandman blinked then turned, watching me. His emotions played across his face like a movie—pain, surprise, and a longing that looked ready to tear him apart. A second later, he shut down his emotional show-and-tell and settled his expression into a look of irritation.

"So Rebel goes off to live in mated bliss, and we're stuck with this asshole?" He hitched his thumb in Magnus' direction.

I snorted and angled my body to face him, subtly turning my back on Magnus. The body language was quiet and subtle, but any shifter who noticed would know exactly what I was telling the useless leader. My allegiance was not to the idiot barking orders.

Sandman lifted the corner of his mouth, his normal cocksure attitude returning in an instant. With a wink in my direction, he inclined his head toward Magnus.

"I'm pretty sure I can take care of myself around here, boss. Maybe you could find a nice, consenting shewolf to handle things for you. They've got to have someone around here who would turn your crank."

"Doubtful." I turned toward the front door to hide my smirk.

Shadow snorted a laugh but didn't comment. Sandman caught my eye, fighting a grin.

"Feel better now?"

"Fuck yes." I straightened my cut, lifted my chin, and rang the doorbell. "Okay, you assholes. Let's get this shit done."

"Notice anything off?" Sandman asked as we waited for someone to open the door. All the shifters in the area would know we had arrived by the sound of our bikes, yet no one had come out to greet us. Even the shifters who'd surrounded us as we drove in hadn't officially welcomed us to Valkoisus land. For a pack, whether they followed the more traditional teachings or not, it was a major breach of protocol. And yet I knew that wasn't what he was referring to.

"No women or pups." I didn't need to elaborate. Sandman let out a quick grunt, letting me know he found the situation odd as well. Before I could give much thought to the atypical behavior, the door flew open.

"It's about damn time you boys showed up."

The man I remembered to be the Alpha of the Valkoisus

pack turned and walked back into the house. No welcome speech or request for respect of pack lands.

I glanced at Sandman then stepped inside. Something on the air, a subtle scent I couldn't describe, teased my senses. I wanted to track it, to find where it was coming from and keep it all to myself. Floral and sweet with a hint of spice, the aroma captivated me and caused the blood in my body to rush south. I adjusted myself as subtly as possible while mulling over what the hell could have caused such a response. I hadn't had a surprise erection since my pup years.

Shaking off the unusual reaction, I refocused on the job at hand and rushed to catch up to the Alpha.

"We came as soon as we received the call about your territory dispute." Sandman gave me a silent *what the fuck* look. I shook my head and kept my eyes on the older man as he led the way through tiled halls toward the rear of the monstrous house. Packs had rules and tended to stand on ceremony, yet the Valkoisus was not behaving in the way we expected. The lack of formality left me feeling a bit off balance.

The Alpha—simply known as Wariksen, if I remembered correctly—chuckled darkly.

"The territory dispute is nothing compared to what these miscreants have done." He led us into the kitchen, which opened to a massive great room with a ceiling three stories high. And a ton of glass and debris scattered about. Some kind of battle had taken place.

Shadow beat me to the question that needed answering. "What the fuck happened here?"

Glancing around the room, I nodded toward a woman in the corner. "Watch your mouth, gentlemen. There's a lady present."

Shadow ducked his head, that strict pack upbringing showing in his submissive posture. "My apologies, ma'am."

"None needed, Breed brothers." The woman approached with grace, her gait long and her body lithe. Her white-blonde hair hung to her hips, and her blue eyes practically glowed against her pale skin as she regarded us with obvious interest. "I am Uuna, Alpha female of this pack. We must impose upon you to help us in more than a simple territory dispute, so your language is of no concern. You will find no censure from me."

I dipped my head, offering her my respect, as was custom in pack culture. At least one person was acting as I would have expected.

Uuna smiled. "Thank you, sir. My husband would prefer to offer the details of this morning."

"They came before dawn." Wariksen looked at Sandman. "Six of them entered the house, but we scented more outside. The cowards snuck in after everyone was asleep. They must have been watching us to know when we bedded down for the night. My guards caught two of them down here. One made it past them, but the other was killed as my pack awoke."

I once again glanced around the destroyed room, taking in the broken furniture and glass scattered all over the floor. Someone had fought hard. Whether that someone was the dead nomad or one of the pack wolves remained to be seen.

"We will help you seek justice for your—"

"Fuck justice," Wariksen interrupted me, spittle flying from his mouth. "They took three of our women from their beds. One mated wolf and a mated human, both staying here as they awaited the return of their husbands from a fishing trip." He closed the space between us, his face a mask of pain and fury. "And they took my only daughter, the Omega of our pack. They have passed the point of justice. I want our women back, and I want the assholes who took them to die by my hands."

Shadow spun and strode out of the kitchen. There was no need for him to speak—I knew he was going to tell Magnus the change in situation. Females of any sort—mated or not, human or wolf—were to be honored and respected. Women who could deal with the animals within us were a rarity, even more so ones born to shift. The rarest of all was the female Omega, who brought a mystical strength and energy to the pack. To have two female shifters in one pack was a blessing. To have a shifter Omega was a gift of the utmost power.

And to have her taken by force was a crime punishable by death.

I looked Wariksen in the eye. "We offer our assistance to retrieve the women kidnapped from your pack. The Feral Breed will not stand for such a blatant disregard for our customs." I glanced around the room, taking in the Valkoisus contingent present. "What's the plan?"

"We are the Feral Breed. We follow no simple pack's plan." Magnus pounded into the kitchen, not even glancing at the Alpha. His tone held no respect, his declaration filled with derision. Knowing Magnus' arrogant attitude toward one of the oldest packs in our territory was a recipe for disaster, I stepped between the two men and addressed my so-called leader.

"Perhaps we should listen to what Alpha War—"

Magnus interrupted me by spitting on the floor. "You growing a pussy now, son?"

I snarled and pushed the little shit against the counter. "What did you say to me?"

"Easy, killer." Always the strategist, Sandman wedged himself between us, directing his full attention to Wariksen as he pushed me away from my prey. "Do you have any idea where this other pack is holing up, or are we going to need to track them?"

I fought against Sandman's hold until he finally met my glare and shook his head. I knew what that look meant…not now. I would get my revenge on Magnus for the blatant insult, but we had Breed business to attend to first.

Fighting back the urge to rip Magnus' head from his shoulders, I relaxed and nodded, giving Sandman the okay to release me.

"They're about fifteen miles northwest of here, hiding out in an abandoned copper mine." Another wolf stepped next to the Alpha, obviously one of his sons. The two were nearly identical. Most humans probably thought they were brothers. "We have a couple of wolves patrolling the woods outside the mine and keeping an eye on the nomads. As soon as we've loaded up the weaponry, we're rolling out."

"We should wait until nightfall." Magnus grunted. "Our wolves will be more focused once the sun sets."

Wariksen crossed his arms and glared at Magnus in obvious disgust, the tension between the two making the hair on the back of my neck stand on end.

"We're going in now, as men. I will not risk the safety of our family by waiting a minute more than necessary. Those beasts brought guns into the camp, so we know they're armed. We have enough firepower here to turn the peninsula into a real island, and we intend to use it to save our women."

Magnus growled deep in his chest, his eyes becoming more amber as his wolf responded to the Alpha before him. "We will fight with honor as wolves. Only cowards would go in with guns."

Wariksen and his son glared hard and stepped closer to Magnus.

"They have weapons and our women. I will not risk any of my pack on outdated posturing. If you want to go in as a wolf once the sun sets, fine. You and your little club can clean up the mess we make as we kill every last one of those fuckers who dared to step foot on Valkoisus territory." Wariksen's voice rose in volume, ending on a yell. His packmates chuffed and yipped their support of their Alpha.

Magnus looked ready to explode, the hair on his arms and face growing as he lost control of his human form and began to shift right there in the kitchen.

"No one tells the Feral Breed what—"

"Per Feral Breed regulations"—Shadow leaned against the counter, completely casual in the face of two powerful shifters about to rip each other apart—"we must bend to the direction of the leader of the pack to whom the women claim allegiance. The only caveats are if the decisions of said pack leader show grievous lack of planning, forethought, or could directly contribute to the death of a Feral Breed member."

Magnus spun faster than I'd ever seen him move and swung at Shadow. I took a step in their direction, but Shadow needed no help from me. He dropped his shoulder as I'd taught him and dodged the blow with a smoothness even I could envy. Magnus' fist crashed instead through a cabinet door.

"You know-it-all little pri—"

"If the dick-measuring contest is complete"—Wariksen's son put himself between Magnus and Shadow—"I'd like to get my mate back from these bastards. She's human, for fuck's sake."

Magnus froze, glaring at the man. Interrupting a fight was a ballsy move, one I could only respect. Most shifters would have chosen to stay clear of a wolf as dominant as Magnus. Wariksen's son, on the other hand, had the stones to confront him directly, even though such an act could be seen as a challenge for position. I knew then, looking between the man I'd been forced to follow and the one I'd only just met, who the true leader was. And sadly, he was not a Breed member.

After several tense moments, Magnus turned toward Sandman and began ranting about being unprepared. The move was meant to be sly, but every shifter in the room knew

Wariksen's son had just bested a leader of the Feral Breed. Magnus had lost any respect the patch on his back had offered him, and sadly, he'd taken the rest of us down with him.

Without a single stutter or smirk, Wariksen's son turned and addressed three other wolves standing guard near what was once a set of French doors leading to a huge deck.

"Is everything ready outside?"

The sentries nodded.

"Fine." He turned and strode over to where I stood with Shadow by my side. "My name is some ridiculous Finnish word my father insisted upon but none of you will be able to pronounce. Call me Rex. We leave in five."

FOUR

WE PARKED THE CARS and bikes about three miles out from a long abandoned copper mine along a stretch of dirt and rock too rough to be called a road. Centuries before, there would have been a bustling town filled with the families of the men working the mines. But, much like me, their time had passed. The area was riddled with abandoned mines and old smelters, often deep in the woods and almost unreachable. At least to humans.

The sun hung high in the morning sky, the only sounds in the still air coming from our team as we prepared for a fight. Late morning was resting time for most wolf shifters. Many would be napping in anticipation of their nighttime runs with the other nocturnal creatures. It was a good time to attack—unexpected. I could appreciate the Valkoisus Pack's desire to go in at this time, as men and with guns. We would likely catch these nomads off guard.

"Think this is going to work?" Sandman asked as he strapped a holster around his broad chest. Two handguns went into the holders beneath his arms, a shotgun held in place on his back.

I loaded the clip in the gun I'd pulled from my saddlebags.

"I sure as hell hope so."

We checked in with the rest of the teams once we were ready to depart. Rex and Magnus had agreed upon a three-pronged approach. The first wave would sneak close to the mine in groups of two. They would be our backup and outliers, ready to move in should the rest of us fail. The second wave would move in teams of four. This was the offensive line, the ones who would take down our adversaries and create a diversion. This would hopefully offer our third group, made up of four Feral Breed brothers, time to retrieve the women and deliver them to the transport vehicles hidden at the end of the road where Magnus and Wariksen would be waiting.

As part of the retrieval team, Shadow and Pup would lead the way into the compound. Where Shadow was super sneaky, almost ninja-like in his stealth, Pup was fast. He could easily outrun any one of us. The two together were perfect for an infiltration—get in unseen and be ready to escape quickly if need be. They would search out the women. Sandman and I would follow the two younger shifters, our goal to infiltrate the den and extract the three women once their location had been identified. As the two strongest fighters of the Breed, we were the best to defend our quarry in case the nomads caught up to us before we could get the girls to the transport vehicle. The second line would be ready to have our backs should something go wrong, but the ultimate goal was to get the women out.

The plan was aggressive yet sneaky, something I enjoyed. The hunter in me was going to have fun with this one.

Once all the teams were in position, I sent Pup and Shadow ahead to the mine. Sandman and I trailed behind them. The rest of our group moved silently through the trees, some in human and some in wolf form to cover all our bases. Most of the others were slightly northeast of our location—each team spread out to fully encompass the property and offer no room for escape.

Sandman caught my eye as we ducked underneath an ancient pine tree. "You ready for this?"

I nodded once and bared my fangs. I kept my wolf close to the surface, ready to shift and take over if need be. Sandman was ready as well. I could see it in the way his eyes burned, hear it as he growled deep in his chest. The Wariksens might not have been our pack, but we were still ready to battle for them and for the safety of the women they cared about.

We were less than half a mile from the mine entrance when all hell broke loose. A single yelp was the only warning we had before the air filled with the sound of wolves growling, barking, and fighting. Sandman and I stayed human, as was part of our plan. If anything went wrong, we would attack as men, fight with guns, and get the women out. No matter the cost.

When we ran into the clearing at the front of the mine, what we saw was a full-on battle. Wolves of all sizes and colors running, jumping, biting, and wrestling. The members of our team that were to remain in human form were on the sidelines, carefully aiming and picking off our opponents one by one. Though the bullets fired probably wouldn't kill one of us without a perfectly aimed shot, they would definitely put the wolf out of commission temporarily. Not to mention, being shot hurt like a bitch.

I didn't envy the shooters—with the amount of wolves in the clearing, it was especially hard to tell which side each wolf was aligned with. The only ones clearly from the Wariksen clan were the snow-white wolves racing through the melee. Those two were sons of the Alpha and could be spotted from two-hundred paces. The rest were harder to identify if you weren't intimately familiar with their wolf form.

Blue smoke suddenly poured out of a small alcove to the west of the main entrance, the signal from Shadow that the women had been located. Sandman and I rushed toward it, skirting the battlefield and avoiding detection. My instincts flared with the adrenaline coursing through my veins, making me feel the urge to shift. I held it back—my body burning in protest, fur sprouting from my skin before I could control it. Get the women out; that was my mission. I would hang on to my humanity until I had done so.

"Incoming!" Sandman's warning came a split second too late. I spun and swung my arm around, but nomad knocked me off-balance. The wolf fell on top of me, clawing and tearing at my back while trying to get his teeth into my neck. I rolled and shoved my shoulder into his gut before reaching up with a half-shifted paw and using my claws to shred his throat.

With a roar, Sandman yanked the now-dead wolf off of me. "You okay?"

I wiped my bloody hand on my jeans and used my clean one to brush the mud off my face. "Yeah, sure thing. Fucker basically tried to mount me is all."

Sandman chuckled as he offered me a hand and helped me to my feet. We continued forward, flanking the opening to the mine. With a quick hand signal, he let me know he would go in first and I should cover him. Seconds later, we were inside, our eyes quickly adjusting to the dark. I yipped once, my signal to Pup that we were close. He came bounding around the corner in wolf form, tongue hanging out, looking like a family pet greeting his master.

"You are entirely too happy, kid." I followed him back the way he came, rubbing at my chest where a strange burning grew stronger with each step.

"You sure you're okay?" Sandman whispered, glancing over at me. He had his handgun out in front of him, ready to fire should another nomad catch up to us.

"Yeah. Just a little..."

The smell of lavender and lime inundated me, making my chest burn hotter and my skin prickle. My knees nearly buckled as I lost all sense of time and space. On the second inhale, my cock filled and throbbed behind the fly of my jeans. I could barely focus as the scent enveloped me in its sensual mixture of sweet and tart.

Four hundred years...

My father had told me the legends of mating—how my fated one's smell would ignite my soul while drawing me near. How I would know before our eyes met that she was mine by the way my body reacted to nothing more than the perfume of her spirit.

I had all but given up hope, been prepared to die alone, but fate had other plans. I was about to meet my mate.

A throaty growl bubbled from within, completely outside of my control. My eyes locked on the turn in the rock and dirt that would lead me to my destiny.

"Oh, fuck," Sandman said as he lowered his gun. "Pup, you better stay with me."

The wolf whined but retreated behind Sandman, neither moving as a deep growl rumbled up from the depths of my soul. My mate would hear it; she would know I was coming for her. She would find comfort in the sound. I turned the corner on tenterhooks, terrified and more excited than ever before at what could lie in front of me.

Three women sat huddled in the corner, Shadow in wolf form standing between them and us. My human mind knew he was guarding them in case our enemies came in before us, but my wolf instincts only saw one thing. There was an unmated male standing in the way of my mate. The roar I let loose was vicious, causing the women to curl away from me as the echo pulsed around us.

All but one.

She stood from behind Shadow, staring right at me with a look of wonder on her porcelain-like face. Without fear, she moved toward me, pulling her white-blonde hair over her shoulder as she walked. I wanted to run to her, to wrap her in my arms and protect her, to kiss her, touch her, hold her, press my body into hers. I wanted to mate with her, fill her with my seed, and watch as my pups grew inside of her.

I wanted her with a single-minded need that left me breathless.

When she finally stood before me, she brought her hand to my cheek. Soft, light…the incongruousness of the gentlest touch and the battle waging outdoors was not lost on me. I whimpered when her skin touched mine, a yearning opening a chasm in my chest only she could fill.

"Gates, we need to get her out of here."

I spun and snarled at Sandman, wrapping one arm around my mate's round hips to pull her behind my body. Sandman stood with his hands up and his head down, subservient and unchallenging.

"She's in danger. We need to get her to her pack—her and the other women. They're not safe here."

My snarl turned into a huff as his words sank in. She needed to go. I had to keep her safe, and that meant getting her out of the cave and away from the people who had kidnapped her.

And then ripping their heads off one by one so they never threatened her again.

"Understood," I said, my voice tight and clipped. For the first time in my many years, I struggled against the wolf inside of me. I needed to stay in my human form, but my wolf spirit wanted out. It was an odd feeling to experience, this separation of self after so many centuries of fluid union.

I pulled my mate around to face me. Her beautiful blue eyes were gentle as they met mine, no sign of fear or worry. As

I stared at her, she began to smile. Her bright red lips turned up just slightly at the corners, as if she were keeping a secret from me.

I wanted to know all her secrets.

"Are you with the Valkoisus pack?"

She nodded, not offering anything else.

"Okay. We're going to get you out of here. Pup and Shadow will meet up with a few men from your pack, and they'll escort you to your home." I glanced over her shoulder at the other two women. "That goes for all of you."

I looked back to my mate and leaned in close, her lavender and citrus scent drawing me in and making me rumble contentedly. I would need to search my memory for pack traditions regarding matings. Whether the Valkoisus was a more traditional or modern pack, there would be rules to follow. History to uphold. Respect to be shown. Erring on the side of a more traditional pack setup, I rubbed my chin along the side of her face, just a quick show of affection before I placed my lips against her ear.

"When all this is done," I whispered, the words long forgotten suddenly coming to dance across my tongue. "I will come for you, my mate. Let me make you safe, and then I will come. The fates have bestowed upon me a bond that I intend to honor. I will meet with your Alpha to show my worth, and I will court you as you deserve. Do you accept my promise?"

I pulled away to look into her eyes once more. They were so wide and filled with wonder. I waited, unsure if she knew the old ways or if she expected a more modern mating. It wouldn't matter to me so long as she was mine.

After several seconds, she smiled and nodded before ducking her head, a pink flush creeping up her chest. I nearly whooped in joy. My mate, my fated one, was blushing at my words.

"You will be safe—I promise you." I shifted my gaze to

Pup, glaring into his lupine eyes. "Anything happens to her, anything at all, and I skin you alive. Do you understand?"

Pup whined and yipped all at once, showing his acceptance and his fear. Every shifter in that dark, dank room knew exactly what had happened, how the beautiful creature and I were now bonded. Only an idiot would cross a dominant male when it came to his mate. Besides, Pup had screwed up when Rebel's mate had needed his protection, and he'd taken his lumps for that mistake. I doubted he would allow anything to happen to a mate of one of the Breed brothers again.

"Ladies, we need to roll out," Sandman said, following Shadow through the opening while holding his arm out for the other two women to join him. I would be taking up the rear, following Pup as he guarded my mate.

The woman I knew nothing about.

"What's your name?" I placed my hand on her lower back and led her toward the opening.

She smirked at me, the curve of her lips both wicked and sarcastic. Her eyes practically glittered in the low light of the cave, every inch of her screaming her excitement. That look, that energy, was the first sign of exactly how much trouble I was in.

"I guess you'll find out when you come for me, mate."

She stopped and lifted up on the balls of her feet as she yanked me down by the armholes of my leather Breed cut. Her lips met mine for the briefest of touches, hot and soft, making every ounce of blood rush to my already-aching cock. That kiss…our first kiss…was better and more arousing than all the other kisses I'd experienced in my long life. It was filled with unspoken promises and hope for the things we'd both been missing. I wanted to whine with frustration when she stepped away.

"Be safe," she whispered before placing another soft kiss

to the corner of my mouth. One final glance at the rest of the group, and then she walked out of the alcove. Her fingers brushed the fur on Pup's neck as he plodded along beside her. I'd never been so jealous of someone else's neck.

I adjusted my cock through my pants and blew out a breath. And then I grinned. I was so fucking screwed, but in the absolute best way possible. I just had to kill a few nomads and wash the blood from my hands before I could go courting.

FIVE

Kaija

I CURLED MY HAND in the fur of the wolf beside me, taking comfort in the feel of the rough strands between my fingers. Though the animal was a stranger to me, I felt safe with him. The past few hours had been the worst of my life, and I wanted to go home to my family and my pack. My eyes drifted to Lanie. The bruises on her face and arms enraged me yet made me feel useless at the same time. Our packsister Helina and I had been unable to protect her from the short nomad who'd batted her around like a tennis ball. They'd called her weak because she cried when they hurt her. I called them cowards for putting their hands on her in the first place.

The wolf at my side whined, so I tightened my grip on the scruff of his neck to quiet him. He was so large for one of our kind, much taller and heavier than a standard wolf. There was no way people would mistake him for one of the wild creatures that roamed our lands. His strength was a force around him, something alive and pulsing. It blanketed me, and I was thankful for his protection. No wonder my mate had chosen him to stay with me.

Mate.

I could still sense the reverberations of the mating bond between us, and I reveled in the knowledge that he stood close behind me. His presence eased the burn of my heat cycle and made it easier to bear. When I'd touched his face and kissed his lips, the pain had receded completely. He was my own personal cooling device, and I looked forward to staying close enough to him to keep the burn at bay.

A tingling along my back told me he was watching me, his gaze traveling the length of my spine. I wanted to turn around so badly, to look into those ice-blue eyes again and remind myself how lucky I was. My mate was gorgeous—attractive to the extreme, like a model walking right off the page, but with enough manly scruff and rough edges to make him approachable. Handsome, well-spoken, and charming enough to woo me with little more than words and the slightest brushes of his skin on mine—I could not have asked for better. Plus he'd shown his respect by telling me he would meet with my Alpha.

I will court you as you deserve.

My heart beat faster remembering the words. I wanted to know more about him. How many years had he lived alone while waiting for me? Why did he ride with the Feral Breed instead of settling in to a pack? Where did he live, and would he be happy on the peninsula with us?

Would he object to me pressing my body against his to rid myself of the insufferable heat radiating from my abdomen?

But first, we needed to reach Wariksen pack land. Lanie needed medical care, and Helina looked exhausted. The strain of the night had taken its toll on all of us, but we wouldn't have to suffer much longer. I had no doubt my father and brothers would be nearby, waiting for us to escape to safety before destroying the animals who'd broken in to our home. I wouldn't have minded a little revenge myself. I owed the short nomad for his rough handling of Lanie.

As we neared the entrance to the mineshaft, the blond man leading the way paused at a bend, light spilling in from the right.

"This is it. Shadow, you're up first with these two." He pointed to Lanie and Helina, who were huddled together in the pool of light. "The Valkoisus pack has their extraction team over the far ridge. Ladies, I need the two of you who can shift to do so when I say go."

Helina nodded. Lanie stood next to her, her eyes flitting around the space as her panic escalated. I reached for her hand and pulled her closer to me.

"They won't touch you again, sister. I promise you that."

She nodded and choked back a sob. The blond man looked up at the noise, and seeing Lanie in a full panic, hurried over.

"Honey, I don't want you to be scared."

Lanie squeezed my hand as tears began to fall down her face.

"No, no. Don't do that." The man hunched down until he was eye-level with the short brunette. "You're going to be fine. Your mate was very specific about how he would dismember not only me but also my entire family if I let a single hair of yours be damaged in this mission. He's creative in his deadliness; I wouldn't want to cross him."

Lanie smiled through her tears. "He can be a little overprotective."

"When you've found the one person who makes your soul sing, there's no such thing as overprotective." He reached for Lanie, and after a pause, she took his hand and released mine. He pulled her under his arm and against his chest. "My name's Sandman, and I won't let anything happen to you, I promise. Me and Gates"—he pointed to my mate—"will get you back to the pack."

Lanie nodded and wiped her face before taking a deep breath. She appeared calmer, which made my heart happy. Rex would have her back in his arms soon enough. I had no doubt in the men who'd been sent to save us.

Sandman held Lanie close as he addressed the rest of us. "Once we turn this corner, we assume everyone is the enemy. Gates, the extraction plans have changed. You're shifting and taking up the rear. I'll stay human to keep our new friend here out of trouble so Rex can get his mate back like I promised. Shadow, you're with me. We need to lead these ladies over the ridge and safely to the extraction team. Pup," he addressed the wolf next to me, his gaze sliding over my face before he clenched his jaw. "Your sole mission, your one goal in life, is to do whatever it takes to keep her alive. There's no room for error here, understood?"

The wolf by my side growled loudly, the hair on his neck bristling. He was awfully brave for a wolf named Pup.

"On the count of three, we shift and run. Ready?" When we nodded, Sandman took one last look around the corner. I glanced over my shoulder at my mate, Gates. He watched me in return, a fire burning behind his eyes that let me know his wolf was close, ready to take over. I couldn't wait to see him in his animal form.

"One."

I pulled my tank top over my head as Helina dropped her cloak. Nakedness was not something we'd been taught to be ashamed of, and yet I felt anxious. I'd never felt so nervous removing my clothing in preparation for a shift as I did at that moment, knowing the man fate had chosen for me would be seeing my naked body for the first time. He'd eventually know every inch of me, but stripping with my back to him made my heart race and the burn in my veins flare.

Once my top was lying in a heap on the ground, I closed

my eyes. Ignoring the sudden tension buffeting my bare skin, I opened my mind to the wolf within, taking a breath as the power surged through me.

"Two."

I stepped out of my pants, reveling for a moment as the cool air caressed my body. I could hear the rumble of my mate's growl behind me, and I hoped it was a good growl. One of want and desire, of lust. Yes, I wanted him to lust after me. I wanted him to desire me as much as I suddenly desired him.

"Get ready."

Ignoring my naughty thoughts about my new mate, I focused instead on my shift. I'd been fighting my need to protect myself in wolf form since my kidnapper had told me he'd hurt Lanie if I shifted. It would be a relief to finally be on four paws. Fur forced its way through my skin, the tingling sensation spreading across my back and over my hips. It was always the most uncomfortable part of my shift. My body morphed from two feet to four so quickly, the bones and muscles barely registered the change, but the fur seemed to take forever.

"Three!"

With a yip, I called upon my wolf spirit and fell into the explosion of light that always signaled a successful shift. The second my paws hit dirt, I ran for everything I was worth. The world flashed by in a blur as I followed the two gray wolves in front of me, one of whom I recognized as Helina. Pup ran by my side, his shoulder brushing mine, keeping pace and growling with every step. I had no idea where Lanie and Sandman were, but I trusted him to take care of her. What he'd said about Rex was true—my brother would kill anyone who hurt his mate.

When we reached the top of the embankment, there was an awful roar, bringing me to a sliding stop. Just below me in the clearing, Gates stood and stared. It didn't matter that I'd never seen his wolf form before; I would have known the look in those eyes anywhere. I would have felt the connection between us from across the globe.

Black as a night with no moon, lean muscle, and deadly confidence, he watched me with an intensity that made me whimper. Everything about him spoke of power and strength—the thickness of his neck, the deep curve of his shoulders, the roundness of his haunches. He was a wolf to respect, one who looked as if he could easily win any challenge thrown his way.

Without warning, a shaggy gray wolf sprang from the tree line, aiming for my mate. Gates pivoted, nearly too quick to see. Teeth bared and bodies tumbling, the two wolves wrestled amidst the brush. The air filled with the sounds of the fight—barks and yips, the breaking of branches and twigs, the thump of one or the other hitting the ground after being thrown off balance. The sight had my heart racing as I realized the danger my mate was in.

When blood bloomed along the bottom of Gates' throat from a well-placed kick, I nearly lost control. My first instinct was to run into the fray, to save my mate. I took a step down the embankment, but Pup jumped in my way. I growled at him as he nipped in my direction, telling me to stay put. I stood my ground, my body shaking with the effort.

My mate was strong and fast. He dodged and lunged, staying one step ahead of the other wolf. The lucky shot to the neck was the only one the gray wolf accomplished, for not long after, Gates had the beast pinned with his jaws wrapped around the offender's throat. Blood poured from the gray wolf, and the animal stilled on the ground, signaling an end to the fight.

A tiny whimper left my lips as I watched the nomad die. Gates looked my way at the sound. It was only a moment, a minor glance between two beings, but it was enough to strengthen my need to be by his side. The mating bond called to me, demanded I join my chosen one. But before I could run down the hill as I wanted, Pup once again stood in front of me, blocking my way. He used his body to push me over the hilltop, away from Gates, away from where I truly wanted to be.

I fought as he continued to herd me farther and farther from my mate. Biting, growling, shoving against him did nothing to alter his course, but I continued. It wasn't until I heard someone call my name that I was able to think of anything other than racing down the hill to stand at my mate's side.

"Kaija, you're hurting him. Please stop!"

Lanie stood in front of me, Sandman wrapped partially around her to keep his body between hers and mine. As I growled at them, the metallic taste of blood registered on my tongue.

Oh no.

I shifted into my human form immediately, rushing to where Pup sat, also in human form. Blood trailed down the side of his face, and scratches littered his arms. All from my teeth and my claws.

"I am so sorry," I whispered, reaching out to brush my fingers over one particularly bad mark. He jerked away and my heart fell. I hadn't thought about whom I was fighting. I'd reacted to the need to get to my mate. I would have chewed through rock if I'd had to, but I hadn't intended on hurting the shifter assigned to protect me.

"You okay, Pup?" Sandman asked.

Pup looked up, his cheeks darkening as his pale green eyes met mine. There was no anger there, only wariness and perhaps a tiny bit of something that looked like respect.

"I'm good, man. Nothing that won't heal by tomorrow." His eyes returned to mine, staring hard. "I think we underestimated you, princess."

"Anyone have a cloak for her?" Sandman yelled.

Pup snorted. "Yeah, before Gates comes up here and kills us

all." He stood slowly, obviously in pain.

"I really am so—"

"Kaija!"

My head spun toward my father's voice. He raced around a stand of trees to my left. I hurried into his arms, almost in tears from the stress and the fight and the relief and the mating. It was all so much.

"Daddy, I hurt him."

"Hurt who, baby?" He pulled me into a tight hug. Someone placed a cloak around my shoulders, covering me. My father adjusted the fabric at my neck before grabbing me by the shoulders to look me in the eye.

"Are you okay? Who's hurt?"

"Pup. Gates needed me." I was shaking at this point, my knees positively weak from the emotional strain of the past few hours. "He was in danger. I was afraid I'd lose my mate before I even got a chance to know him."

"Your mate?" My father's eyes widened. "You're mated to one of the bastards that took you?" He roared in his fury.

"No, Daddy. Not one of them. The shifter, Gates. He came to rescue us."

"Gates?" He looked over to Sandman. "Which one is Gates? Please don't tell me it's that sniveling little fucker you brought with you."

Sandman grinned as he brought Lanie toward us. "Gates is the dark-haired man who came in with me; he's the Sergeant-at-Arms for the Feral Breed Great Lakes den. He's a good man, honorable and upstanding. He'll be a strong and loyal mate for your daughter."

"Yes, I think I remember." His forehead furrowed as he watched me, though what he was waiting for, I couldn't have guessed.

A howl went up from behind us, breaking the relative

silence. Everyone tensed until two loud yelps followed.

"Let's go." My father grabbed my arm and pulled me away from the howl, away from Gates.

"Wait! What about—"

"That was the signal to fall back to the house. Two yelps means success, so your mate should be fine. But there could be more nomads in these woods, and I don't want to take any chances. The Breed members will stay and search out any stragglers." He looked over my shoulder as one of my older brothers raced up the hill. "Bernte, take Lanie. We'll need to let Rex know she made it out before he claws a hole in the earth searching for her."

"I already sent the message with Kasen." His eyes met mine for a moment before hurrying over to give me a hug. "Don't ever do that to me again, little sister."

I pressed my face into his cloak, taking comfort from his familiar smell. "Okay."

He pulled back and held me at arm's length for a moment, inspecting me. When I had passed whatever set of criteria he was looking for, he nodded and switched his attention to Lanie.

"I'm sorry we failed you, sister."

Lanie's eyes grew huge as she stared at my brother. She swallowed before replying, "It wasn't your fault."

Helina joined the two in a quiet conversation, her hand never leaving Lanie's arm. My poor sister was about to be the most protected pack member ever to walk Valkoisus land. I hoped Rex could handle all the extra attention on her.

Hearing what sounded like another fight breaking out across the clearing, I searched out Sandman. The thought of Gates being injured made my stomach turn. I needed to know he wouldn't be alone. Before I could even ask Sandman to watch out for my mate, he grabbed my hand and looked me in the eyes.

"I'll find him right away. And once we rid the world of these nomad cowards, I'll bring him to you."

"You'll make sure he comes home?" I asked, my voice shaking. Sandman's eyes tightened, a frown cutting across his face before his expression went blank.

"No wolf gets left behind in our club. I'll make sure he's okay and bring him...to your pack."

SIX

Gates

"FUCK ME."

"Pretty sure you should be saying that to the pretty, white wolf, my brother. Not to me."

I rolled my eyes at Sandman as I reached around to check the damage on my shoulder. The shaggy wolf had gotten a lucky break when he caught me staring after my mate. I shouldn't have allowed the distraction, but her snow-white coat and the way she ran so gracefully had caught my attention. Plus, as much as I loved my Breed brothers and trusted them, she was my mate. There was a deep need within me to take care of her. I'd followed the group far enough to keep her in my sights, and the fucker had caught me looking. It was a lucky break. Still, he wasn't lucky enough to keep breathing once I was done with him.

"All the boys check in?" I asked as Sandman walked up behind me. I hissed as his rough fingers prodded my broken flesh, but I didn't move away. Pain was good; pain meant healing.

"You'd have to ask Magnus since he appointed himself point person on this mission."

"I'm really getting sick of that little fucker." I winced as he hit a particularly painful spot.

"Hmm, he got ya good." Sandman came around to stand in front of me. "C'mon man, let's go find the guys and get you cleaned up so you can spend a little quality time with your new mate. Forget about den bullshit for a while."

I grinned. It was automatic and unstoppable as thoughts of my mate swirled in my head. I was going to look a bit deranged when we finally joined back up with our team, but I didn't care. This day was supposed to be about battle, about bravery and vengeance and damage done. My mate had turned the purpose of the day around at first glance. Through the pain and the dirt and the death, I had found something utterly precious and made of joy.

"I don't even know her name yet."

Sandman smirked. "I do."

He tossed me the clothes I'd quietly taken off in the mine entrance. Watching my mate strip for the first time had damn-near been a religious experience. All that pale skin, all those soft curves. I'd barely been able to hold myself back from taking her right there on the dirty, rocky floor. I wanted to hurry through cleanup so I could come to her. I would need to prostrate myself before her father to show my respect, but hopefully he wouldn't make us court too long before we could begin our Ritcs of Klunzad. Three days alone with a woman who had a body like hers? Sounded like heaven to an old iron-horse rider like me.

Once I was suitably covered in jeans and my cut, we jogged over the embankment and down toward the scene of the main altercation. Men in various stages of undress cleaned up the evidence of the fight. Many of the pack wolves had worn their cloaks, but most of my brothers had simply stripped before shifting. Some had shifted on the fly, meaning there were a few naked asses running around. Happened every time. Hopefully they had extra clothes in their saddlebags.

"So what is it?" I finally asked when Sandman's smug silence got under my skin. "What's her name?"

"Oh, hell no, I'm not telling you." He laughed and turned toward where Magnus stood. "But I'll give you a hint. It's fitting for her wolf and in her ancestral tongue."

"Ancestr...what? Why can't you give me a straight answer?"

"What fun would that be?" He kept heading toward Magnus as I stopped next to Rex and a group of the Valkoisus pack.

"I don't know many Finnish names!" I yelled after him. "How the fuck do you know her name anyway?"

He laughed again. "Because I know stuff. Plus, I'm old and shit; history is kind of my thing."

"I'm older, you cocky bastard."

He was smiling and flipping me off when the first wolf hit him, having jumped clear over the top of the rock outcropping. Two more followed, completely covering him in seconds. I shifted in the middle of my first running step, going from boots to paws in the blink of an eye. Three other wolves, none of them from my den, came out from a far corpse of trees, running flat out toward where Magnus stood.

I ran as hard as I could, barking to give Magnus a heads up as to what was coming his way. He and Sandman both needed help as either could easily be overpowered since they were so outnumbered. But Magnus had a number of pack wolves nearby, and Sandman had me.

I raced across the forest floor, barreling straight into the pile of wolves attacking my Breed brother. Gunshots sounded through the air. I didn't pause to figure out where they were coming from. I couldn't stop fighting. Sandman lay in wolf form under the pile of biting, clawing animals. Not moving... not fighting back. As my teeth sank into the neck of the first aggressor, a wolf who smelled like Rex flew up beside me, and then came Shadow into the mix. The three of us battled hard, forcing the wolves off Sandman and creating a protective circle around him. He was our brother, a true Alpha in every way that mattered, and we would protect him to the death.

Without warning, all three nomads shifted to human form. Two of them moved to flank the one directly in front of me, the one with the most power in his stance. I shifted as well, being the highest member of our pack with Magnus down. Shadow stood at my side while Rex stayed in wolf form, hovering over Sandman. A handful of members of the Valkoisus pack circled around the back of the nomads, trapping them.

I addressed the one I assumed was the leader. "You realize you're outnumbered, outgunned, and completely out of your league, don't you?"

The man laughed. "Your little motorcycle club affiliation has made you cocky, whelp." I growled as he smirked at me. "Cocky wolves make mistakes, and wolves like the ones we work for like to take advantage of mistakes."

"What's that supposed to mean?"

"It means you'd better keep a close eye on that pretty, white bitch you took from us. Boss man seems to have a special interest in her; sent two teams out here just to make sure we captured her."

My growl grew louder, the need to rip apart this threat to my mate nearly making me lose my mind. But I held my ground. If my mate was in trouble, I needed to know as much information on the who and the why as I could.

"Why would he want her?"

He snorted. "Because she's an Omega. He has a special... fondness for Omegas. And he has yet to add a white one to his collection."

My stomach dropped as I glared at the stranger. Collection.

This wasn't a one-time incident, it wasn't a territory dispute, and it wasn't over. Somewhere, other packs were missing the women these assholes had stolen from them. Somewhere, our honored Omegas were being held against their will.

Without warning, the stranger leapt forward. I edged one foot back but allowed him to grab me by the throat. "He will come for her again, and there's no way you can stop him, cub."

Rex growled ferociously, rocking on his paws. He must have thought the nomad actually had a shot at beating me. Shadow, on the other hand, stood beside me, a wicked grin pulling up one side of his face. He knew me well after the past few years of working together, knew many of my strengths and weaknesses. And he knew this fucking animal would pay.

"You really have no idea who you're dealing with, do you?" Shadow chuckled darkly and raised a single eyebrow. "You've just gotten yourself a dance with the Gatekeeper, fucker."

The nomad's eyes widened for a split second, but that was all the time he had. With a twist, I wrapped both arms around his and yanked, breaking the bones above his elbows. His scream was cut short as I spun him around and slit his throat with my claws. Shadow leaped on the man on my right as I lunged for the one on my left. One roll, a single mistake on his part, and I had my arm wrapped around his throat.

I leaned in close to my prey's ear, whispering so the Valkoisus wouldn't hear. "No one threatens my mate." And then I ripped his head from his body.

As soon as Shadow had his target neutralized, he raced for Sandman. Rex shifted, looking a bit green as he stared at the headless shifter.

"Damn, man. Where'd you learn to do that?"

I wiped the blood off my face and spat, ridding my mouth of the flavor of my opponent. "I'm four hundred years old, *man.* I've fought for five different countries in seventeen different wars. Where do you think I learned it?"

He chuffed and shook his head. "Remind me never to fuck with you, old man."

"Consider it done." I walked over to Shadow, who knelt next to Sandman. Rex hovered nearby, keeping watch over our fallen brother in case any more nomads tried to go for our weakest link.

"What's the verdict, doc?"

Shadow snorted. "I'm a medic, not a doctor. Sandman's pulse is good, and the damage the other wolves inflicted is healing nicely—all except for a massive goose egg at the back of his head. He must have hit a rock on the way down, which would be why he's unconscious."

"So basically he gets attacked by three wolves and the most damage is done from a rock on the ground?"

"Pretty much."

I shook my head. "Figures." I leaned down to take a good look at Sandman. Shadow was our team medic and the one with the training to help in situations like these, but I hadn't lived this long without learning a thing or two. I needed to see him alive and breathing for myself before I could move on. Sandman's skin was a healthy color, his breathing even, and his skin knitting back together where the other wolves had clawed him. I figured three hours and he'd be back to his usual cocky bastard self.

"We're going to need to help him out of here."

"What can I do?" Rex asked. "Should I call back my team? Or that Pup guy?"

I shook my head. "No. I don't want my mate left with so little protection."

The shifter looked completely gobsmacked. "You have a mate?"

Rex's question made me pause. For the first time in my

very long life, I could answer that question in the affirmative. And yet, Rex was her brother, and I was uncomfortable talking about my mating with him before I spoke to their father.

"Kind of." I turned away, an uncomfortable burning sensation in my chest. I hadn't lied about my mate, but my words could have been seen as disrespectful or, in a worst-case scenario, a mate refusal. I would need to pull Rex aside once I spoke with Wariksen.

Shaking off my discontent, I refocused on the situation at hand.

"I can hump Sandman out of here. We just need to find Magnus."

Shadow pointed behind me. "Last I saw, he was fighting off two wolves near that tree line."

I stood and headed in the direction Shadow indicated. "Rex, stay with Sandman. Shadow, let's go find the boss so we can get the fuck out of here."

Once we were away from prying ears, Shadow chuckled. "Anxious to spend a little time with a certain female, are we?"

I grinned, couldn't help it, the thought of being alone with my mate making me happy, horny, and proud.

"I have much to do, brother. I need to officially come to her Alpha and make my courting request, and then I need to talk to Rex and explain why I didn't tell him about the mating just now. Once those things are done, I will begin the traditional courting rituals."

"Wow. I don't think I've ever—"

His words failed as we came upon the site where a fight had obviously occurred. The leaves were tramped into the mud underneath; hundreds of paw prints pushed them into the murk, creating a sea of leafy mud. The brown mess was splattered with blood, some smelling of Magnus. But there was no sign of him.

I spotted a piece of paper pinned to a tree across the field and hurried toward it. Shadow reached it first, handing the paper to me as he glared into the trees.

"I know he's not the strongest leader, but I didn't think a couple of nomads could take him down. It looks like he put up one hell of a fight, though."

I read the note, my blood turning to ice in my veins as the words sank in. Something was wrong...very, very wrong. And it seemed my new mate was stuck in the middle of it.

"What's it say?"

I handed him the note, too busy sorting through memories in my own head to reread the thing for him.

"One by one or all at once, you all go down if we don't get the white Omega. Bring her to us, or your Alpha dies." He glanced at me. "But we don't have an Alpha."

"They mean Magnus." I grabbed the note out of his hand and strode toward where Sandman lay. He was one of the smartest, most strategic wolves I'd ever met. More so than Magnus. Nearly as strong as Rebel. Quiet but intelligent. If anyone could help me keep my mate safe, it was the man currently knocked out on the forest floor.

"Call the Fields. Blaze needs to know what's happened. And then call every other Feral Breed den President. I want to know of any and all issues concerning Omegas in the last five years."

Shadow nodded. "What about Magnus?"

I kneeled down and wrapped my arms around Sandman's hips and shoulder, turning and hefting him into a fireman's carry. My quads burned as I pushed into a standing position, but I didn't have time to go slow. My mate was in danger, and I needed to set up a team to make sure no one could get close to her. With a grunt, I adjusted Sandman on my shoulders and walked up the hill toward the road where we'd come into the forest, Rex and Shadow following closely.

"Magnus is on his own right now. There aren't enough of us to track him, and we have no idea how many wolves are in this nomad cluster. We need to regroup and plan what to do next, but for now, we need to figure out how to deal with the shitstorm coming our way.

SEVEN

Kaija

"KAIJA, SIT DOWN ALREADY," my mother said from across the room.

I huffed but continued pacing. Gates had yet to return, and I was anxious to lay my eyes on him.

Lanie came to stand next to me. "It's never easy when they're away."

I looked into her eyes, seeing the residual fear and anxiety there. Lanie was a good kid, a sweet girl who had come to the peninsula for college. One chance encounter at a grocery store, and she was family. Had those nomads taken her from us, we all would have been inconsolable. I needed to thank Sandman for making sure she escaped safely.

Ever the sensitive one, Lanie reached out and took my hand, squeezing hard. "They'll be back soon. Do you feel the bond between you yet? Can you tell where he is?"

I closed my eyes and focused on the mating bond. It was definitely there, a little tug pulling me north. But it was weak, either from the newness or from the fact that we had not yet claimed each other as mates.

"Barely."

"Well, barely is better than not at all." She stood beside me at the window, watching the driveway for any sign of cars or wolves.

A few moments later, the sound of an engine drawing near pricked my ears. "They're coming."

Wolves and human mates seemed to appear out of thin air, all walking outside to welcome our family and new friends home. I stood at the back of the group, wringing my hands. Pup came to stand beside me, ever watchful.

When the first truck made the turn onto the driveway, three of the women behind me rushed forward, knowing their mates were in the vehicle. This continued as more trucks arrived, mates and children, parents and friends running to greet their heroes as I stood watching and waiting.

Finally, after most of the wolves had retired inside and there were only a handful of us left on the porch, two trucks pulled into the drive. My father was in the first one along with a few of the men from the Breed. I grew worried when I didn't see Gates in the second truck, but I knew he was nearby. I could feel the pull to him, the strength increasing every second.

"Kaija," my father yelled as he opened his door. "Get the doc."

My heart dropped to my feet and tears burned my eyes. Someone was hurt. Where was Gates? What would I do if—

"Baby." My mother placed a hand on my shoulder. "Do what your father says. Now."

I nodded once, reluctant and terrified, but followed her instructions. I ran through the house and out the back door, shifting on the fly the moment my feet touched grass. My red cloak floated to the ground behind me as I raced away, the fabric like blood on the green carpet of the earth. Turning my head, I shook off the feeling of dread and increased my speed. Within moments, I was at the door of the pack doctor, an older

Anbizen, or turned wolf, by the name of Booth.

He was on his doorstep when I arrived, apparently waiting for me.

"I am needed?"

I chuffed, quick and direct. He nodded and grabbed a bag before following me to the house on foot. By the time we reached the yard, everyone was inside. I shifted human, my body aching and my bones sore from both my heat cycle as well as changing form so much. While shifting was not necessarily painful if one kept the right mind-set, repeatedly switching from wolf to human and back again could be harmful and was definitely exhausting. I grabbed my red cloak from the grass and clasped it around my neck on my way in the door. The familiar slide of the fabric around my hips and ankles offered a comfort I needed at that moment.

We entered through the porch doors and hurried down the tiled hallway where, only the night before, Chinoo had cornered me. It seemed like a lifetime had passed since those moments, yet it had only been a matter of hours. Important ones for sure, but mere hours nonetheless.

Walking into the great room, I kept my eyes moving, scanning for Gates. Seconds that felt like hours passed as I looked, desperate for a glimpse of his black hair, needing to see those blue eyes once more. The longer I looked and didn't find him, the more my heart raced. He wasn't there. He hadn't made it back. Chest tight and world spinning, I took a step toward the front door. My knee buckled instantly, nearly taking me to the floor. But a warm hand caught my elbow before I could fall.

"Easy there." Gates stood in front of me, covered in blood and mud and the gods only knowing what else, but he was there. Alive and relatively unscathed. Eyes burning and relief washing over me like a balm, I hurried to embrace him.

"Kaija."

The sharpness in my father's tone made me stop.

"I spoke to Mr. Gates on the way back from the mine. One of the Feral Breed is injured, and there is much still to do in regards to these nomads. I know you were expecting more from him, but for now, your mate is choosing not to come for you."

A collective gasp went up from the shifters watching the exchange. If it were possible for my heart to stop beating, it would have. There was no bracing for the level of pain that swamped me. Every dream I'd had, every hope of a happy life with my fated mate crashed. My face and neck burned with the humiliation of having so many of my packmates hear my rejection. My mate did not come for me. He would not be bonding with me.

He did not want me.

I couldn't look at him, didn't want to be near him any longer. With a short nod to my father, I turned and raced for the stairs. There were too many eyes and ears in that room. Too many people witnessing my shame. I needed to escape. I ran up the stairs to the second floor, desperate for the solitude and privacy of my suite.

"Please stop."

I froze as my heart faltered and my head fell forward. Gates' voice echoed down the hall, soft yet forceful. Even though he'd just rejected me in front of my pack, I couldn't resist him. My cheeks burned as I tried to will myself to walk away from him. I'd embarrassed myself and my family enough. I'd assumed he would want a mate as much as I did, that when he said he'd come for me and court me, he meant it. I'd been hopeful, and losing that hope was devastating.

"Do not run from me, Kaija. Things are not as bad as they seem."

"You did not come for me." I shook my head, my eyes burning with unshed tears. "You said you would come, but you did not. You don't want me."

Gates reached for me, his hands shaking and slow as they crossed the unspoken line between us. I didn't move, didn't pull away or lean in. I simply stood as a statue, my eyes staring at the toes of his boots. When his hands finally grasped my skin, I shivered. The mating call was loud and intense, my heat cycle not helping the way my body yearned for him.

"Don't." The word was a growl as it crossed my lips. Gates froze. I lifted my chin and glared at him, heat and want and lust all swirling together inside me. The passion I felt for him was quickly turning to rage—for being dismissed, for being lied to, even if only for a moment, for losing the only dream I'd ever had.

"You don't get to touch me if you're denying me."

"I am not denying you." Gates' voice was barely above a whisper, but his eyes held mine in a strong stare.

"Then why did my father say you didn't come for me?"

"There are things going on that make it inadvisable for us to move forward in our courting."

I crossed my arms over my chest. "What things?"

"I... I would rather not worry you."

"I am not a child." I pulled away. "You don't need to sugarcoat or hide information from me. If our mating is inadvisable, I expect to know why. I won't stand for dishonesty from anyone in my life, least of all some drifter who rolled in to town and now seems to be bent on playing with my emotions."

Gates growled, the sound causing a shiver to roll up my spine. Warmth spread out from my lower belly, my nipples hard and my panties wet from nothing more than the rumble vibrating through the air.

"Will you not listen to me?" Gates asked. He stepped into my space, forcing me back against the wall and pinning me in place. "I'm not playing with your emotions, nor have I been dishonest. I wanted to come for you tonight. I would have gladly begun our courtship this very night or our Klunzad, if you so desired. But those men who took you aren't all gone, and your abduction wasn't random."

I shivered as his breath washed over my face. "What do you mean?"

His fingers traced up my arms. "Whomever they work for wants you, my white Omega. And while we managed to… dispatch some of them, there are more who got away. You're not safe. I won't risk you further by beginning our courtship while they lurk in your woods."

I reached up and grabbed his arms, sighing at finally making the contact I so craved. My breasts pressed into his chest on every breath as he leaned into me, practically hunching over to account for our height difference.

I trembled as he breathed me in. "My pack can protect me."

"They failed you once." He dropped his head to my shoulder, slowly nuzzling into my neck. "I won't allow that to happen again. My Breed brothers and I will protect you."

"And if I don't want that?" I gasped as his lips met my jaw.

"Then you'll be a very unhappy princess until we capture the bastards coming after you." He leaned back, his ice-blue eyes meeting mine. "I've waited many lifetimes to find my mate. I won't allow you to be at risk."

"But I'm safe here."

"Not safe enough." He pressed his hips into mine, the hard ridge of his erection rubbing against my hipbone. I responded in kind, loving the way his eyes grew more intense with each pass.

"And how do you propose to increase my security? Will you station your brothers inside my suite? Will they be forced to follow me as I go about my daily routine?" I pressed my face against his chest, clinging to the leather vest he wore to hold me upright. His smell was intoxicating, completely masculine and arousing.

His growl deepened. "No other men will be in your room, princess."

"Then how?" My lips dragged across his collarbone as I moved my head from side to side.

"I don't know yet." He ran his hands up my arms, soft and slow. "How did they get in your room?"

"The one came through the patio door from my balcony. The other from this hall."

He pulled away, brushing the sweetest, gentlest kiss across my lips. "Then it looks like I'll be making my home on your balcony. And I'll place one of my men outside your doors to guard from this side."

He drew me close, the beating of his heart pounding against my chest. "I won't let them get to you again. And when I have ensured your safety, I will begin the courtship as I promised. I am a man of my word, young one. I will not disappoint you."

HOURS LATER, AFTER RETURNING to the great room and listening to my father rant and rave about how I would be safest with a pack guard, to which Gates argued vehemently, I climbed the stairs once again on my way to my suite. The one they called Pup walked a step behind me. He'd apparently drawn the short straw to be stationed outside my door.

"This is a bit much, don't you think?"

"If Gates thinks it's necessary, then no. Nothing is too much to keep his mate safe."

"My pack is aware of the danger. They will patrol and guard the house. You aren't going to do any good standing in the hall." I paused at my door and turned to scowl at the young shifter. His intense expression forced me to pause.

"I failed a brother's mate once, and she and I almost died because of it. I will not fail again." He pushed open the door and directed me inside. "So as Gates' mate, if he tells me to stand here all night, I'll stand. If he tells me to fight, I'll fight. If he tells me to play fetch, I'll play fetch. Because if anything were to happen to you, he would never recover."

I took a step back, my brow furrowed.

Pup blew out a breath. "He's been alone a long time, longer than any other unmated shifter I know of. God only knows how he's lived as long as he has, but one thing is for sure. Finding you may very well be the thing that keeps him alive. So whatever it takes to keep *you* alive, I'll do. Because in all the ways that matter, he's my brother in all the ways that count, my family beyond club brotherhood or pack bonds. I carry his blood in my veins." He leaned in, his eyes hard and his face serious.

"I will not fail another mate."

I stared into his eyes. They were so strong, so filled with determination. They left me no room to doubt his intentions.

"Understood."

He smiled and stepped out into the hall. "Go to bed, princess. Your prince is waiting for you on the balcony."

The second the door was closed, I spun and raced for my bedroom, excited to once again see Gates. Though I still wished we could have begun our courting, I was beginning to understand his fears. I would want to lock Gates in the attic with me if I thought someone was after him.

My patio door was open, a cool, soft breeze wafting through the curtains and bringing the lemony-sage smell of my mate along with it. I fought back a smile as I purposely ignored the open door.

If my mate thought I was going to ignore the fact that he was so close to me yet I was unable to touch him, he was wrong.

I hummed as I sat at my vanity, letting my scarlet cloak fan around me. I brushed my hair, making sure it hung light and shiny over my shoulders. When I was done, I stood and walked to my hope chest. I dug deep for the box of sexy lingerie I'd long ago hidden, biting back my grin. I pulled each item out, holding it up and inspecting it as if to determine what to wear to sleep. But tonight was not about sleep. I wanted to tease my mate. And I was, if the rumbles coming from the balcony were any indication.

When I pulled the last item out and found it unsatisfactory, I stood and untied my cloak from around my shoulders.

"You wouldn't." Gates' deep voice carried into the room, the tone dark and filled with desire. I liked it. I wanted to hear it again.

"Wouldn't what, dear mate?" The ribbons holding my cloak together at my neck hung free, and I slipped one shoulder out of the billowing fabric.

"You're not wearing anything under that robe."

"It's a cloak, not a robe. And of course I'm not wearing anything under it. Cloaks make for easy shifting." I glanced at the patio door over my shoulder. "Are you concerned you'll see me naked again? The whole pack has on numerous occasions. It's hard to be modest when you're transforming your body into another species."

"I'm not concerned, per se." The wind blew a little harder, lifting the curtains and giving me a glimpse of Gates. He stood in front of the open door, his hands against the screen, his eyes dark and hungry as they watched me. "I'm more interested in preserving the sanctity of the ancient mating rituals. I've made our mating bond public; I'm not supposed to see you naked before I officially come for you and your father approves the union. If you disrobe, you'll be breaking the rules."

"The rules don't say I can't be naked," I slid my other arm

out of the fabric and allowed it to fall just enough to show the tops of my breasts. Gates sucked in a breath as I slowly walked toward the open door. Once I reached it, I pushed aside the curtain and placed my hand against his where it pressed into the screen.

"The rules say nothing of the mated female hiding her nudity. It would be near impossible given the nature of our shifting." I leaned forward as Gates matched my movements. Our noses brushed through the screen, breath mingling and hands pressing harder against one another. With a sigh, I pulled away and turned my back on my mate.

"The rules only say the mated male is to avert his gaze when nudity is required." I dropped my cloak and stepped over the pool of scarlet fabric. "I assume your gaze is averted?"

"It's...something."

I smiled. "Good boy. My heat seems to be coming early, and my body aches from that, plus the stress of all the shifting today. Any sort of nightwear would make me more uncomfortable than I already am."

As Gates' growl grew louder, I climbed onto my bed and crawled across the mattress. I moved every part of my body in a deliberate fashion. Swinging my hips, rolling my shoulder to turn in such a way as to show him a hint of my breast. I could practically feel his eyes on me as I teased him. The sensation ramped up my heat, burning me from the inside and making my body ache with a need I was unfamiliar with. I groaned when I finally slid between the sheets.

"Are you in pain, princess?"

"A bit, but it's nothing I can't handle."

"I'm an old shifter, my sweet. Should you need relief from the irritation of your heat, I may be able to assist you."

I turned and met his eyes through the screen, loving the way his more formal words aroused me. "I will not be bedding you before our courtship, Gates of the Feral Breed."

"There are more ways to ease an unfulfilled heat cycle than just…sex."

Sex. The word rolled off his tongue seductively, making my skin tingle in anticipation. Licking my lips, I ran my hands down my stomach to rest on my hipbones.

"What are these ways?" My voice came out husky and warm, even to my own ears.

"Are you asking for my assistance?" Gates slid his hands up the screen as his eyes bored into mine.

"No. Just curious, really." I grinned as he dropped his head against the screen. "Why? What are you offering me?"

Gates lifted his head, his eyes meeting mine once more in a stare so intense, I could practically feel it like a weight against my chest. "When you're past the point of curiosity and need relief, I'll show you."

"Tease."

"Right back at you."

I giggled, knowing he was right. "Goodnight, my mate. Thank you for respecting the rules and allowing me a hint of modesty as I made myself comfortable in this big bed."

Gates chuckled and stepped away from the screen. "It was my pleasure, princess. Sweet dreams."

EIGHT

THE FAMILIAR RUMBLE OF engines roaring through the still, morning air startled me awake. I jumped to my feet with a snarl, instantly alert and ready to protect my new mate, but the sound was too far away to be an immediate danger. Though it was coming closer.

I stretched out the kinks in my back from sleeping on the hard balcony floor and then peeked inside. Kaija lay curled in a ball under her blanket, still sound asleep. Which was good. Yesterday had been traumatic for her, and rest would help her mind settle. She needed time to heal. And with her coming into heat…fuck. I sniffed, the warm scent teasing me and making my morning wood even more pronounced. Sweet, feisty, gorgeous beyond reason, and smelling like sex? She couldn't have been more perfect.

I watched her sleep for a moment before scanning the room to be sure nothing had changed while I'd rested. I knew Pup would be in the hall on the other side of her suite doors, so I wasn't overly worried about anyone coming in that way. The balcony and patio door were the weak points in her net of protection. I would have preferred if she'd slept in a room internal to the house, one without windows and with only one door. I could protect her better then. She could hole up in our cozy den, and I could keep myself between her and the door. Safe.

But I had a feeling Kaija would hate that. She wasn't meant to be hidden away; she was too bright for the dark.

The pack shifters were making themselves known, going about their daily life in camp. I could see three of Wariksen's guards from my perch and knew he'd assigned more for the perimeter of the house. Feeling confident that Kaija was safe for the moment, I whistled to Pup to let him know I was leaving. He responded as expected from inside the house. My Breed brother would guard her for me; of this, I had no doubt.

With only a single backward glance at my resting mate, I hopped over the balcony railing and raced for the front of the house. I hoped the short run would burn off some of my frustration. Kaija was naked and in heat, I was hard and desperate to feel her underneath me, and there was nothing I could do to quell the ache that had settled between my hips. Fucking nomads and their shitty fucking timing.

Sandman was on the porch when I reached the front of the house, no lingering signs of the bump he took to the head the day before. I leapt over the railing and hurried to his side. Rex soon joined us, coming from inside. He wore jeans and a T-shirt, no cloak this time. He would have fit right in with our Breed crew if he'd been wearing the leather vest Sandman and I sported. The thought of him in Breed colors struck me hard. He'd be an asset to our team.

Other than a few grunts of greeting, there was no discussion between us. There was none needed. People were coming, and we would protect the entrance to the house until we knew if they were friends or foes. We formed a blockade to the front door and stood guard, the three of us ready to meet our visitors.

Within a matter of minutes, four motorcycles turned onto the wooded drive of the pack camp. Smiling from the lead position, Ray-Bans in place and arms up to reach his ape-hangers, Half Trac glided onto the asphalt patch running along the side of the house and leading to the garage. When he turned off his engine, he didn't stand up. He just sat on his bike, facing me. Waiting me out.

I returned his stare, unwavering and stoic. There was no way I'd let Half Trac win a contest. Even one like this that was for fun. I'd known him too long to back down from one of his games.

Finally, after several uncomfortable minutes of silence between his group and ours, he grinned.

"Jesus, man. When Shadow called, I thought for sure I'd be coming up here to light your pyre because that karma bitch finally caught up to you." He swung his leg over his bike and crossed the distance between us. "I sure as shit didn't think I'd be coming to help you with a case that involved your *fated mate.*"

"Karma's got nothing on me, my friend." I stepped forward when he reached the porch.

Half Trac didn't falter as he approached me. As soon as he stepped within striking distance, he gripped my forearm with one hand and pulled me into a back-slapping hug.

"How are you, brother?" I asked as I backed out of his hold.

"I just spent twelve hours in the saddle, fucker. My ass hurts, my legs ache, and I need to take a piss. But fuck me, let's chat about this whole mate thing."

I laughed and nodded, pulling Half Trac off to the side of the porch for some relative privacy.

"So it's true? You found your mate in the shifter Kaija Wariksen?"

I ran a hand through my hair, fighting to hold back the grin

I felt spreading across my face. "Yeah, it's true."

"Damn, man. Fate doesn't fuck around. Not only is she a Wariksen, so I can assume she's blond and gorgeous like the rest of them, but she's also an Omega?" He whistled low. "You are one lucky SOB."

"I'm not feeling so lucky right now, man." I shook my head and settled a hip against the railing. "These nomads are after my mate, and they're using a Breed brother, a leader, to bargain for her life. I don't know what to do to get Magnus back while keeping Kaija safe."

Half Trac glanced at the two men behind me. "Magnus is not the biggest piece in this puzzle, not by a long shot. We have much to talk about, old friend. How's about we head inside? I'd bet Uuna has a pot of coffee on for the boys, and I wasn't kidding when I said I needed to take a piss."

We were halfway to the front door when Rex asked, "What about them?"

The "them" he referred to were the three wolves with Half Trac. A team of Cleaners. Feral Breed members but without the loyalty or respect for the club the rest of us had and without a den designation rocker on their back. More nomad than the rest of us, Cleaners danced on a razor-thin line between feral and man-eater and helped the Breed with the more delicate missions. They had a high level of skill for body disposal, hostage retrieval, and were armed with creative ways to kill the people who needed killing. They also refused to listen to anyone but Blaze.

Half Trac turned and looked at Rex before indicating the Cleaners with a tilt of his head. "They're not exactly house-trained."

Rex raised his eyebrows and glanced at me. I shook my head, fighting the sense of unease the new additions to our team brought on before leading Half Trac through the door.

Rex followed, leaving Sandman outside to babysit the Cleaners.

"Dear, sweet Uuna." Half Trac raced across the kitchen to wrap the smiling Alpha female in his arms. "It's so good to see you. You're looking even younger than the last time I had the pleasure of your company. How is that possible?"

Kaija's mom smiled. "Always with the compliments. I see you're still trying to charm your way through life, Seamus."

Half Trac—or Seamus, apparently—gave me a glare over Uuna's shoulder. Real names were rarely shared among the club. Some of the guys within a den would probably know a member's given name, but that information was kept secret. Once a man made it past hanger-on status, he was known as Pup. He kept that name until he'd earned his full patch or been kicked out. Patched members always went by road names. It was a sign of disrespect to use a member's given name after they'd earned their cut. I wouldn't be using the Seamus moniker anytime soon.

Cups of coffee in hand, our group moved through the house toward the porch. Half Trac and Uuna led the way, with Rex and me bringing up the rear.

"So, you're mated to my sister."

I stopped mid-step and regarded the shifter. I knew this conversation was coming, but with the mission the day before and Kaija misinterpreting my delay in finalizing our mating, I hadn't yet had time to address her brothers as I knew needed to be done.

I looked Rex in the eye and stated simply, "Yes."

He stared at me for a long moment, not speaking or moving. And then he nodded once.

"You'll do."

I frowned as he walked past me. *I'd do…for what?*

With a huff, I hurried after him. "That wasn't quite the answer I was expecting."

Rex shrugged. "It's fate, man. What do I get to say about it? When I met my Lanie this past winter, nothing and no one would have kept me from her. And trust me, fucking bad energies tried their damndest. But I got the girl in the end, and I'd kill anyone who tried to get between us." He glanced at me with a smirk on his lips. "You're old enough to know how fucked-up some of the traditions in packs are, you're smart enough to argue with my father without getting clobbered, and you're strong enough to keep her safe. Welcome to the family. Don't piss off my mom."

I choked on my coffee and sputtered. "Thanks, I think."

We'd just turned from the hallway into the main foyer when the Cleaners whooped from outside. Rex paused and looked toward the door.

"You think they can help us?" he asked on a whisper.

I shrugged. "Maybe. Though Cleaners represent a whole different kind of danger. They're not exactly known for their manners."

Rex snorted. "Kaija will be more than happy to teach them a few, I'm sure."

I was stepping onto the porch when I heard the voice of the woman in question. Kaija stood at the bottom of the porch stairs, surrounded by the three Cleaners. The situation appeared to be no more than a simple conversation, but then Kaija jerked back as one of the men yanked on a lock of her hair.

My shift was instant and unstoppable. I dug my claws into the wood decking of the porch as I raced for my mate, my mind a haze of hate and blood and need to protect what was mine.

"Gates!" Half Trac jumped in front of me, wrapping his arms around my throat and throwing his weight against me. I fought his hold, biting and clawing any part of him I could reach in my desperation to reach my mate. We tumbled to the wood floor in a mass of fighting, snarling flesh. I arched and rolled and snapped, grunting when Half Trac's legs wrapped around my hips and pinned me down.

Suddenly, Alpha Wariksen stood in front of me, a glare in his eyes. "You will stop now, son."

For the first time in nearly three hundred years, I'd been Alpha-ordered. The force behind the words pushed past my mindless rage. I didn't want to obey him, but I knew I needed to in order to quell the fury flooding my system. With defeat souring my mind, I stopped fighting and lay still on the porch.

Rex had Kaija off to the side of the steps. He'd placed himself between her and the fucker who'd dared to touch her. Knowing she was safe helped me calm the rage within, and with only a minimal pause, I was able to shift to my human form.

As soon as Half Trac released me, I jumped up and stalked to the Cleaner who'd dared to lay a finger on my mate. My fist met his jaw as soon as my feet met dirt.

"Touch her again, and I swear to you, I will bleed you dry slowly."

The fucker smirked as he wiped the blood from the corner of his mouth. "Big talk from a neutered dog."

With a roar, I lunged, but once again, Half Trac held me back.

"Easy now."

I growled and struggled against the man's hold but to no avail. I was too filled with rage to fight smart, and Half Trac knew it. We were a pretty even match when fighting, but my single-minded desire to protect Kaija gave him a distinct advantage over me at that moment.

The Cleaner laughed as he watched my struggle. "Can't even get away from the master's pet, can you, mutt?"

He stepped into my personal space, his nose mere millimeters from mine. "You think you're wolf enough to handle that bitch? She stands here practically in heat, reeking of want, and yet you do nothing. I can't even smell you on all that creamy skin she's hiding."

I growled and glared, ready to kill the motherfucker for his disrespect. He just licked his lips.

"I'd be more than happy to ease that heat for her." He grabbed his crotch crassly as he took a step back. "I've got more than enough to settle the little bitch's problems since you can't seem to find your nuts."

Half Trac's arms tightened as I once again lunged for the filthy beast.

"You come near her, and I'll make sure you never walk again."

"Gentlemen, I do believe it's time to stop." Wariksen stepped off the porch, his arms crossed and a deep scowl on his face. "Might I suggest a fifteen minute cool-down period before we begin the planning? There is the problem of a missing Breed member and a crew of wolves coming after my daughter."

I glared at the Cleaner for another few seconds before nodding. The Alpha was right—there were bigger problems at issue than one handsy near-nomad with a filthy mouth. Besides, the camp was spread over a lot of land with plenty of woods and clearings to disappear into. I'd get my revenge on the fucker soon enough.

Resigned to being patient in my plans for revenge, I turned toward Kaija to make sure I hadn't scared her. Her wide eyes were focused well south of my face, a becoming, pink blush high on her cheeks. Her chest rose and fell in a quicker rhythm than standing warranted, and the smell of her heat dripped through the air like warm honey. My mate must have liked seeing my protective side. And my naked body.

"Kaija." Uuna's voice had Kaija jumping and whipping her head to the left. "Gates is in need of new clothing. Why don't you take him upstairs to get him one of Rex's cloaks?"

"Yes, ma'am." Kaija ducked her head, a flush on her sweet cheeks. I strolled onto the porch behind her, not at all uncomfortable. Kaija led the way up the stairs and down the hall in the opposite direction of her room. Eventually she opened a door to what appeared to be a walk-in closet filled with linens and cleaning supplies. Once we'd walked inside, I shut the door softly behind me. The tight space and nearness of my mate made my ever-present erection grow harder, something I probably should have been embarrassed about.

"You can look at me, you know." My voice came out soft. I didn't want to scare her; I wanted her to be comfortable around me, no matter what. She was my mate. Soon, I hoped, she would be intimately familiar with every inch of my body, as I would be with hers. There was no need to be embarrassed because of a little skin.

She took a deep breath, her back still to me.

"Kaija? There's no reason to be embarrassed."

She snorted a laugh. "I'm not embarrassed to look at you, Gates. I've grown up in this pack and seen naked men every day of my life."

"Then why won't you face me?"

"Because if I look at you, I'm going to want to kiss you. And if I kiss you, I'm going to want to throw you on the ground. And if I throw you on the ground, we will start our mating right here in this closet. Rules and danger and overhearing parents be damned. So please, put a cloak on before I lose control of myself."

I came up behind her, looming over her shorter frame and brushing my cheek against the top of her head. "What if I want you to lose control?"

She whimpered, the sound going straight to my cock. I stepped forward, guiding her against a wooden shelving unit, pressing my chest along her spine and holding her in place.

"What if I want you to look at me? Would you do that? Would you get a good look if it was what I really wanted?"

Her hands came around to grip my hips, pulling me close, my erection pressing into the softness of her ass.

"Yes."

"Then turn around, sweet girl. See me. Get your fill before we're forced back outside by the responsibilities standing between us."

She spun slowly, pressing her luscious body against my ever-hardening cock the entire way around. I growled low and long. Her touch made me burn with a desire so deep, it took everything in me to keep myself in check. Soon I would get to touch her. Soon I would get to taste her. Soon I would have my cock buried inside her wet heat. If I could only be patient.

When she faced me, I took a single step back. Then another. And finally, one more. I stood tall and proud before her, my feet planted shoulder-width apart and my hands on my hips. Her eyes roamed my face before she slid her gaze down my neck and over my chest. My abs. My hips. My cock.

Her look spoke of hunger, deep and dark and sultry. I knew her need. I felt it as well. And fuck, did I want to ease both of our suffering.

"You're so beautiful." Her words were a whisper, barely heard over our ragged breathing. She took a step toward me before reaching out with a tentative hand toward my aching erection.

"May I?"

The only response I could muster was a soft groan as her fingertip slid along the head of my cock.

"How is something so hard also so soft?" She continued down my shaft, her touch gentle and tentative.

"Oh hell, Kaija." I bit my lip to hold back a howl as she wrapped her fingers around my length and squeezed. Her eyes met mine, all wide-eyed innocence with a hint of seductress peeking through.

"May I?"

This time I nodded, unable to make a single sound beyond the constant rumble in my chest. Her hand encircled my cock, gliding up and down along my length. I couldn't take my eyes off the picture—her small, pale hand wrapped as far around me as she could reach, sliding, rubbing, twisting. Oh gods, the fucking twisting.

"Princess," I gasped as she added her other hand to my length, the two working me in opposite motions. Never before had I enjoyed a simple hand job so much. Never had I been as turned on. I was about to embarrass myself in front of my mate, and I was loving every second of it.

Kaija continued to work my cock as she dropped to her knees. She edged closer, her bright red cloak fanning around her on the floor. When her ruby lips were mere millimeters from the head of my cock, she looked up at me with those big blue eyes, this time filled with pure sin.

"May I?"

I released a growled "Yes," the only communication I was capable of. Thank the fates it was enough for her. In the next second, those bright red lips were wrapped around the head of my cock, sucking hard as her tongue teased the underside of the head. Deeper, faster, wetter...she pulled me in deep, all the while moving those goddamned hands around my cock in a rhythm that made me shudder. Minutes, hours, who cared—my mate was sucking my cock, and it was fan-fucking-tastic.

"Kai...I'm gonna...fuck."

She increased the twisting of her hands around my shaft and pulled more of my cock into her mouth. I whimpered and shivered from my head to my toes, unable to stop myself from wrapping my fingers in her hair. Heat and wet and friction and the sight of my mate on her knees before me pushed me right over the edge. She felt so good, looked so much like a fantasy come to life. There was no stopping my pleasure. I came with a full-body shudder, my hands gripping her head, her name falling like a prayer from my lips.

She licked me from base to tip as I stood before her, shocked and blissed out and still shaking from the force of my orgasm. I'd come faster than a teenaged boy watching dirty movies for the first time. And though I probably should have been embarrassed by that fact, I wasn't. My girl certainly didn't seem to mind as she licked and suckled my softening cock. I whimpered when she finally released me, my skin missing her touch right away.

She gave me a wicked smirk. "Happy, mate?"

I merely nodded my assent as she rose to stand, all that red fabric hiding her body from me. She pressed herself against me, the fullness of her breasts teasing me from beneath her cloak. Soft. My girl was so fucking soft.

"And Gates?" Her breath blew across my lips as I leaned over her.

"Yes, princess?"

"When it's my turn, I want you to know that my answer will always be 'Yes, you may.'"

NINE

GATES HELD MY HAND all the way down the stairs on our return trip to the front porch. It was a sweet moment, a tiny bit of affection after such a lewd act. I still didn't know what had come over me. Whether it was seeing him naked…so very naked…or being alone with him in that tiny, private space, or if it was another effect of my heat cycle, something had made me want to throw him on the floor and have my wicked way with him. For hours. Or days. So long as we were naked together, the duration wouldn't matter. I craved his touch and his attention, and he seemed to reciprocate my desires.

He stepped in front of me at the door, opening it with a wide swing of his arm. I walked onto the porch with a smile. Gates smiled back at me, all blue eyes and full lips. I wanted those lips on mine. Wanted to feel the way they moved over my flesh. His cloak billowed around him as the breeze picked up. A pack cloak with our insignia on the sleeve, the dark maroon color to denote him as a mated wolf of the Wariksen clan. My mother glanced at the two of us, and a smirk spread across her face. She knew I'd chosen his cloak color intentionally. I may not have been able to have my Rites of Klunzad yet, but

I was certainly going to let everyone know the man was mine. Unavailable. Taken.

Claimed.

"Kaija, can you please let Collette know we will need the far west cabins opened for our new guests? These gentlemen will be tracking the nomads and would prefer to stay out of the main camp."

"Of course, Mother." I glanced at Gates, but he wasn't looking at me. His eyes were focused over my head at the group on the grass out front. And he was glaring.

"I would prefer if she didn't go alone." Gates' voice rumbled from his chest, deeper and darker than normal.

"Collette and Dante live just beyond the tree line." My father pointed to where the peak of the cabin my brother and his family shared was visible through the pines. "We'll be able to see her the entire way. And our guards are stationed around the property. No one will get close to her, young Gates."

My father's voice held an edge of Alpha, making his request feel more like a command. Gates stared at him for a moment before dropping his gaze to meet mine.

"Be quick."

I shivered under my cloak at the steel in his voice. That was not the look of a happy man. I had no idea, though, what had happened to make him so angry since we'd walked outside.

With a nod and one final squeeze to his hand, I left Gates on the porch and descended into the crowd. One by one, the men stepped out of my way, though slowly and with more effort on my part than normal. I heard Gates' growl as I pushed through the crowd but didn't look back. Something in the air was making me anxious, and I wanted to get away as quickly as I could.

It took nearly thirty minutes for me to walk to Dante's cabin and deliver the message. It wouldn't have taken so long but I couldn't tell Luka no when he asked me to color a picture with him. And while thirty minutes wasn't nearly enough time with my nephew, it was a long time to be separated from my new mate. At least, it seemed that way. I needed my mate, practically itched for his touch as I hurried down the path leading to the lawn of the Alpha house.

I crested the hill onto Alpha property, my eyes immediately scanning the yard for Gates. He sat with his friend, Sandman, and a large group of Breed and pack men. I grinned as the sunlight shone on his inky hair, bringing out blue highlights I hadn't noticed before. So handsome. His eyes met mine as I walked across the grassy field. A wide smile bloomed across his face when he saw me heading his way. It was such an automatic response, such a natural reaction to seeing me that I nearly lost my breath. My eyes locked on his, both of us grinning like fools. A love story told in a single look.

I passed one of the guards on my way to reconnect with my mate, not realizing it was Chinoo until he spoke.

"You're making a fool of yourself."

I noticed Gates' frown as I turned and glared at my packmate. "I have no idea what you're talking about."

He canted his head in Gates' direction. "That biker trash over there. You're walking around all googly-eyed and love-struck when he's already refused you."

My back stiffened, and I nearly hissed at him. "He did not refuse me."

Chinoo laughed, deep and dark and absolutely infuriating. "Sure he did. The whole damn pack knows he didn't come for you, even after you two felt the mating bond. All this 'it's only because of the danger' crap is just that. Crap. Once those bikers get their leader back, they'll ride off into the sunset, and you'll still be waiting up on that balcony like a sad, lonely Juliet jilted by her Romeo."

"You're wrong." I moved to leave, but he grabbed my arm and spun me around.

"Don't walk away from me, Kaija. You're beautiful, feisty, and you smell like sex from your upcoming heat. Almost every unmated wolf in this pack would give their right paw to fuck you right about now. And yet, he hasn't bedded you yet, has he?" He leaned close and sniffed. "But every wolf over there knows what the two of you were doing when you were supposed to be retrieving a cloak for him. We can smell it on you. He'll let you suck his dick, but he won't mate with you. You're just too stupid to see the truth; he doesn't want you."

I fought to hold his gaze, but something in mine must have betrayed me. He tightened his hold, bringing his face closer as his smirk turned cruel.

"He'll tell you all the pretty words you need to hear, but in the end, his actions speak the loudest, don't they? Good enough for a blow job in the closet, not good enough to bond with."

I shrugged even as my heart cracked at the thought of being rejected. "Maybe he doesn't want me. Maybe he's just here to do a job and will walk away as soon as it's over." I jerked my arm out of his grasp and pinned him with my harshest glare. "But until that time, I'm going to treat him as a mate deserves to be treated. I'm going to smile at him and spend time with him. And every day, multiple times a day, I'm going to offer him pleasure. He is my mate, and I choose to treat him as such."

Chinoo growled, his expression murderous. I ignored his growing temper and flipped my hair over my shoulder.

"Besides, pleasuring him"—I wiped the corner of my lips with my thumb and smirked—"is no hardship for me. He makes it worth my while when we're alone. The man has seriously talented fingers. And his mouth! Sweet mother of nature, I could ride his face all day long and never tire of the feel of his tongue against me." I sighed and smiled, selling the lie as well as

I could, before scowling at him once more. "But what happens between my mate and me is none of your business. If he rode off tomorrow, I still wouldn't lay with you."

"Fucking whore," Chinoo spat before he lunged. I dodged and spun, striking with my left leg as I planted my right. The kick connected exactly as I'd planned—a solid shot to the middle of the chest. Chinoo flew backward, past a smirking Gates and a chuckling Sandman.

"Everything okay over here?" Gates asked as he strolled to my side. I brushed a lock of hair out of my face and huffed.

"Peachy. I was just explaining to Chinoo here how what we do in the bedroom—or outside it, as displayed earlier today—is none of his concern."

"I like your communication methods, princess. Very effective." Gates leaned down and brushed a sweet kiss across my lips before pulling back to look me over. *You okay?* he mouthed. I knew I could say no. The way he stood blocking me from Chinoo spoke volumes. He was giving me the chance to ask for help without losing face in front of my packmate. One word on my part, and Gates would jump in to rescue me. And yet, I didn't need his rescue. I'd taken care of Chinoo on my own, and I wanted to savor that feeling. So with a smile and a shrug, I nodded.

Gates kept his eyes on mine for a beat longer than normal before he gave me a single head bob.

"Isn't that cute." Chinoo struggled to his feet. "Your white knight's come to your rescue once again. I guess that's what growing up as the adored princess of the pack will do to you—make you weak." He smirked at Gates. "Pretty sad how helpless she is, man."

Gates laughed, throwing his head back. Long and loud and full, as if Chinoo had just said the funniest thing in the world. Chinoo watched him with a wary, uncomfortable expression.

"Helpless? I watched her plant your ass halfway across this field. I would never call her helpless. Besides, I wasn't coming over here to rescue her. I was just making sure she had a getaway ride"—his voice dropped to a growl as he stared pointedly at the younger wolf—"in case she killed you."

Chinoo choked and sputtered before turning and walking away at a fast clip. The coward.

Gates wrapped an arm around my shoulder and pulled me into his hold. "Which reminds me, Sandman and I have a meeting with the Cleaners and your pack leaders. How about we head out for a little run as wolves before the meeting starts? Just you and me."

He stared down at me, his eyes filled with a heat that made my heart race.

"That sounds perfect."

WE RAN THROUGH THE woods along the trails leading to the houses of various packmates. Weaving in and out of trees, following in the footsteps my ancestors had tread for hundreds of years. The air rushed by, ruffling my fur and bringing with it the sounds and scents of nature around me. I loved the land I'd been raised on, loved the freedom the relatively remote location brought us. Even in the depths of winter, when the cold and the snow battered the peninsula and forced the humans indoors, I loved to run across the terrain as my wolf. There was nothing like the feel of fresh powder under my paws and a brisk, icy breeze teasing my nose.

Gates ran right behind me, his black-as-night wolf following me over the hills and across the flats. When we reached a heavily wooded section not far from the coast, I turned to go around, but Gates yipped and led me to where three pine trees had grown closely together. Their bottom boughs hung heavy, creating a kind of cave under the branches. Gates led the way inside, and then shifted into his human form.

I whined, the sight of his naked thighs making me want to follow his lead and shift, but he shook his head.

"I want to talk to you, beautiful. And if you shift, you'll be naked. And I'm naked. And that's not quite where I want this conversation to go. At least not yet."

I huffed and spun, racing out of the den he'd found and across the grassy field. He yelled after me, but I didn't stop. I ran all the way to the edge of the hills where my brothers and I had often played as children. Inside a hollowed out tree trunk were three cloaks. The pack kept them scattered about the land in case we needed them, though none of us was particularly uncomfortable with nudity. Clothes were more of a hindrance than a necessity most of the time, but one never knew when humans would wander onto our land.

I pulled a cloak from the pile with my teeth and ran back the way I'd come, returning to the little pine den my mate had found.

"Smart girl." Gates smiled when I rushed in, tan fabric in my mouth. I dropped it in his lap and curled up next to him, his thigh brushing against my fur. He wrapped the cloak around his hips and sat back against the center tree trunk.

"I heard what Chinoo said"—his eyes met mine—"and I saw your face. I don't want you to think that my not coming for you yet is a sign of rejection. If it weren't for these nomads putting you in danger, we'd be deep in the Rites of Klunzad right now. But I can't lose my focus and put you at risk."

I sat up and faced him, eye to eye with the man who would be mine. His eyes turned dark and intense as he stared into mine, his face serious.

"I have waited over four hundred years for you. A few more days to make sure you're safe is nothing in comparison." He fisted his hands in the fur around my neck. "Please don't believe someone as obviously jealous as Chinoo. He knows nothing of my intentions."

Unable to take the pained look in his eyes, I shifted to my human form, scrambling into his lap with my legs on either side of his hips.

"I believe you. When this is all over, we'll have our three days to bond. And I'll give myself to you fully, as you'll give yourself to me."

He nodded, his eyes locked on mine. So soft, so filled with emotion. I leaned forward and placed my forehead against his.

"And before the three days are over, we'll exchange our mating bites and tie ourselves together forever."

Gates growled deep in his chest. I'd always been told of how the idea of exchanging the sacred bites would excite the males of our species. I didn't know if that was true for all, but it definitely worked with Gates. His eyes practically glowed with a lustful fire as he hardened underneath me.

"You want to exchange mating bites right away?" His voice, normally so smooth, came out rough and dark.

I slid closer, pressing along his erection as I adjusted my position.

"More than anything."

He practically whimpered as he pulled my hips toward him.

"I want that too. So much."

Without a second thought, I crashed my lips to his. He responded in kind, quickly taking over the direction of the kiss. His hands gripped my ass, rocking me over his dick. I wiggled until the hardness pressed where I wanted it, where every slide made me gasp and shiver. We continued that way for what felt like hours, me writhing naked in his lap, him kissing me breathless.

My hands explored every dip and curve of his muscled body

I could reach. From the strong cords running down his neck to the hardened peaks of his nipples, the light hair scattered across his chest to the rippled plains of his abdomen. I happily ran my hands and fingers over his flesh as we kissed and rutted and breathed each other's breath.

"You have tattoos," I whispered as my eyes caught the faded amber ink across his collarbone. I followed the foreign words with my fingertips. "My crazy life, yes? But you switch to English for this one."

I placed my hand against the word "Trust" on his ribs, feeling a scar my eyes couldn't see in the shadows of our little pine-tree den. Our hips slowed as he watched me watching him, our movements measured and sultry instead of fast and frantic as they'd been. The change in rhythm made me growl and shiver as pleasure rippled up my spine.

"That's it, princess. Feel me." Gates licked the length of my neck, pausing only to place gentle bites along the way. I dropped my head forward as tingles shot from my toes to the top of my head. The feel of his body against mine, even with the irritating fabric between us, was so much better than anything I'd experienced before. Every brush of his skin against mine brought equal parts pleasure and relief from my heat.

Gates groaned and pulled me down harder against his straining dick.

"Fuck, I want to see you come." His words made me moan, my head falling as I worked my hips harder, snapping them back and forth. My breaths came in pants and my thighs burned, but my orgasm was so close, the tension so strong. I just needed a few more minutes. A few more slides. A little—

With a growl, Gates flipped us over. The sudden roughness of dirt and pine needles against my back caused my eyes to fly open. Gates hovered above, holding himself up with his arms, peering at me with unmasked desire.

"I want you so much, Kaija. Not just like this." He thrust against me, angling his hips to slide the head of his dick from the bottom of my opening to the top of my hood and back. "I want you to be mine, forever. I'll take care of you. I promise. I'll always make sure to keep your happiness in mind. Just please give me a little time. Let me clean up this nomad mess. Trust that I'll do right by you."

I reached up and fisted my hands in his hair, pulling his face down to meet mine.

"Yes, yes, yes. Always yes, my mate. Always." I pressed my lips to his before arching into his touch.

He growled and dropped his head to my shoulders, thrusting harder and faster against me. The thin cotton of the cloak did little to keep us apart, the fabric wet and rough as it kept him from going where we both wanted him to be. A few more thrusts and I was teetering on the very edge of desire, ready to fall over. But I couldn't quite get there. I needed just a little more, a little something, a little push—

On a gasp, I bit down on the side of his neck, my body locking down as the taste of his skin kicked off the biggest orgasm of my life. Every inch of me shook, every muscle clenching and releasing in time with my pussy. Gates hissed and thrust harder, no longer able to keep a rhythm.

"Fuck, fuck, fuck, Kaija. Fuck." He groaned, loud and long in the silence of our pine-tree den. He arched and threw his head back as he came, beautiful in his release. I wrapped my arms and legs around him, pulling him into my embrace as soon as his high began to wind down. I needed to feel him—his weight, his heat. I needed him to be real, to be with me. To be mine.

"Baby." His whispered endearment was followed by a brush of his lips and a nuzzle of his nose. "So beautiful. So ridiculously beautiful."

"I feel the same way."

He chuckled and dropped his forehead to rest on my chest. "This wasn't my intention, you know. I just wanted to talk to you."

"I like the way we talk. We seem to not be able to keep from *talking* when we're alone." I grinned as he pulled his head back and smiled at me. "Besides, we did talk. I heard you, Gates."

He sighed. "My real name is Luke. Well, technically that's not true. My original name, the one my parents gave me, is Lorenzo Martinez de Caballero. We shortened it to Luke when we moved into the United States, or what was the United States at the time."

"Then why does your team call you Gates?"

"It's called a road name." He rolled, taking me with him. "We all have them. It's a way to bond with the brothers of the club. There's a whole process to joining the Breed, but once you're through the majority of it, you're given a road name. Sometimes it has to do with something you did, like Shadow, who's one sneaky SOB in wolf form. Other times it has to do with something about you. There's a man in our club named Rebel. We call him that because he was turned during the Whiskey Rebellion, fighting the government over taxes on whiskey."

"On whiskey?"

He chuckled. "Yes. It seems ridiculous now, but back then, whiskey was a way to make good money for farmers. Rebel didn't take too kindly to the government trying to get a cut."

"So why are you Gates?"

"Because I'm the gatekeeper, the protector. Even before I was named Sergeant-at-Arms of our den, I was the one making sure our clubhouse was safe and secure. Most of us live in what used to be offices in our den on the north border of the city. I protect the den and my brothers within."

I pressed my lips together as I tried to make sense of his words. "You call them brothers, but they're not."

He nodded. "The Feral Breed is a brotherhood of men fighting the same fight. We have to be more than friends… In our jobs, we must trust each other with our lives. No simple friendship is enough. Though I do have an actual brother. His name is Beast, and he's close to two hundred years younger than I am. He's the reason for the tattoos."

"No other family?" My heart ached as his face fell.

"All the rest are dead."

"I'm sorry." I snuggled into his hold and rested my head against his chest. "I'd like to meet this Beast."

"Then you will. Once we're done here, we can head to the Lower Peninsula and I'll introduce you to him." He ran his hand down my arm and over my hip, clutching me in a way that spoke of possession. "People are, at times, a bit afraid of him."

"He's your brother; I won't be afraid. I'll treat him like I do you, and everything will be fine."

He growled. "Not exactly like you treat me."

I grinned as his lips met mine. "No, not exactly."

He kissed me hard, stealing a few more moments of privacy before we had to leave our den and return to the Alpha house… and the danger circling the pack.

TEN

AFTER GRABBING A SECOND cloak from the hidden stash—bright red this time, quite obviously one belonging to the Alpha clan—Kaija and I strolled to the main house. The talk had done us good, as had the two rounds of intimate play. I felt more connected to her than before. It'd broken my heart to see the doubt and pain on her face when that fucker used my protective instincts to imply that I didn't want her. She was funny and beautiful, witty and smart, and the fates had chosen her as the perfect match for me. The pack wolf she'd fought with was completely cracked if he thought there was any way I wouldn't want her. I wanted her like the sun wanted to shine or the tide wants to roll—constant and unable to stop.

When we reached the yard leading to the house, the scene before us made me pull Kaija closer to my side. My Breed brothers stood on the porch as if waiting for me, Half Trac a few feet in front of them. Wariksen and Uuna stepped out from around them as well, all watching our approach.

"Do you think we're in trouble?"

I shook my head and squeezed Kaija's hand. "No. I think something's happened and we won't like it."

We slowly approached the porch, waiting for someone to begin the conversation. Finally, after we stopped at the bottom of the steps, Half Trac addressed us.

"The nomads have sent a message through one of the Valkoisus packmates they saw in town. We're to meet them tomorrow morning."

"What do they want?"

Half Trac's eyes darted toward Kaija before landing on my face. It was a tiny tell, a slight change most people wouldn't have noticed. I not only noticed it, I read the intention behind the move. They wanted Kaija. My chest burned and my joints ached as I fought the urge to shift and protect her.

"No." The voice that came out of me was not my own. It was a sound of pure rage, of fear and desperation forcing my soul into the deepest, darkest corners. It was the voice of a wolf warrior balancing on the knife-edge of reason

"What? What is it?" Kaija asked as she looked back and forth between her parents and me.

Uuna lifted her chin, the wet shine of her eyes the only outward sign of her inner emotional turmoil. I growled as her eyes met mine, making the Alpha step in front of her and attempt to stare me into submission. But this was about my mate, my one true match, and I would not back down to anyone when it came to her safety.

"No."

"You have no say in this, young one." Alpha Wariksen approached until his chest nearly brushed against mine. "You two aren't officially mated, and therefore your opinion carries no weight."

My neck and ears burned with the fire of a level of hell I'd never reached as my hands curled into fists. "Fuck you and your antiquated rules. No."

Wariksen roared. "How dare you speak to—"

"She is my mate, and I will say—"

"Stop!" Kaija stood at my side, pulling me away from her father. "Please, Gates. Tell me what's going on."

Uuna grasped Wariksen's arm and tugged him back as I gripped my hair and roared my frustration. Fucking nomads and their fucking bad timing and my fucking need to keep Kaija safe. Had I just thrown her down to the ground and fucked her in that cave the first day, we wouldn't be in this situation. I would be in a position of power in regards to her as my mate. Most pack Alphas respected that power and wouldn't push a mated pair into anything they weren't comfortable doing. But Wariksen was right. The fact that Kaija and I were not yet officially mated took me out of the equation when it came to her. I could rant and rave and suggest all I wanted to, but in the end, her Alpha made the call.

Sandman stepped in front of me, his expression a mess of pain and anger with a hard-fought confidence trying to break through. "They want to exchange Kaija for Magnus. They say if we don't agree, they'll burn the Wariksen's out of their camp after they come for the human mates."

"They can't do that." Kaija's voice was soft, slightly shaky. I wrapped my arm around her shoulder and brought her against my side.

"You told them to go pound sand, right?" I asked on a growl, knowing the answer.

"They will destroy this pack." Wariksen pointed at me from where he stood with Uuna, his face red and his voice too loud for the distance. "They will take the land we've lived on for hundreds of years and break the Valkoisus apart bit by bit. Our mated wolves will leave the pack to protect their mates."

Sandman nodded at the Alpha before looking from me to Kaija and back. "There have been three other Omegas go missing in the last two years. One from out east, one from Texas, and the third from a small pack in northwestern Canada. No one put the pieces together because each case appeared independent, plus the Breed doesn't always know what's happening in other territories. These guys slipped through our cracks and now have three of our beloved Omegas. We need to capture at least one of these nomads if we have any hope of finding those girls."

"Fuck." I dragged my hand down my face and threw my head back. I wanted to scream. I wanted to claw down the stars and let them set fire to the land. I wanted to rage against the fates, that they would give me the greatest gift then threaten to take it away from me. But most of all, I wanted to run. Grab Kaija and leave.

Which made me no better than all the mated Valkoisus wolves who would abandon their pack to protect their mate. A particularly sobering thought.

"We need her cooperation, Gates." Half Trac took a step closer, his eyes on mine. "We'll keep her from harm, but she has to be a part of our plan if we have any hope to capture the men who threaten her future."

I looked down at Kaija. She peered at me, her blue eyes calm and a small smile on her red lips.

"I'm not afraid. My pack needs me, as do my Omega sisters. I know you and your Breed brothers won't let anything happen to me."

She stepped into my arms and wrapped her little body around mine. She suddenly felt so small, so breakable. And yet, I'd seen her strength the past few days. I knew she could take care of herself. But that didn't mean I had to like putting her in danger's path.

I clung to her, afraid to let her go. "I cannot lose you." My voice was a whisper, barely audible. But she heard me.

"I'll never leave you. Besides, you'll all keep me safe," she murmured with her lips against my collarbone. "And when this is all over, I will come for you. And I will court you as you deserve." She tilted her head back, a saucy smile on her face even as her eyes spoke of the level of fear she felt.

I forced my lips into what I hoped was a smile and swallowed hard. "I think that's my line."

Her smile fell, her face turning serious. "So tell me. Not tucked away in a private spot, but here. In front of your Breed brothers and the leaders of my pack. Say the words, Lorenzo. Make me yours."

Her request awoke something inside of me, something hot and primal. My mate wanted me to make it known that she was mine. Something I should have done from the start. I should never have allowed her packmates to wonder if I would refuse our mating or if I wanted her to be mine. I should have lifted her up in front of her pack and hollered my joy at finding my mate for all of them to hear. I should have done so many things for her. But I couldn't go back in time and correct my mistakes. All I could do was move forward, progress through life, learning as I went.

Never looking away from her, I bent at my knees so I could stare straight into her eyes. With as much conviction as I had in me, in a voice loud enough for even the guards at the tree line to hear, I repeated the words I'd said to her in the cave.

"When all this is done, I will come for you, my mate. Let me make you safe, and then I will come. I will meet with your Alpha to show my worth, and I will court you as you deserve."

She smiled and nodded, her eyes glassy with unshed tears. "I am yours, Lorenzo. And I will wait as patiently as I can for you."

Without warning, I lifted her into the air and twirled her in a circle. Her red cloak swung out behind her, and her light hair made a wave of white above the jewel-toned fabric. She was the brightest star in the sky making up my life, and I wanted nothing more than to bask in her light forever.

My brothers were whooping with joy when I finally set my girl back on solid ground. She ducked her head against my chest, her shy side showing itself as the Feral Breed members surrounded us. They gave me pats on the back and placed their hands on her arms in welcome, a traditional gesture ingrained in all of us. Kaija smiled and nodded, offering thanks and appreciation for their welcome. And when my brothers were done and she stood in a semicircle of Feral Breed men, Kaija surprised us all with her bravery and directness.

"Well then, let's get this plan rolling. I have a mate waiting for his chance to woo me." She turned toward the porch, meeting the eyes of her father. "I'll do what you've asked of me. I'll assist in saving the Breed leader, and when he is safe, I'll help with the missing Omegas case. I won't allow this pack to be torn asunder, and I will not abandon my Omega sisters."

Her mother nodded once, tears falling down her face. Apparently I wasn't the only one scared out of my skin by Kaija's bravery.

"WILL YOU BE BACK tonight?"

I tasted Kaija's lips again, quieting her. My hands slid along the skin of her back, hidden from anyone who happened up the stairs by the awfully convenient cloak she still wore. The draping fabric gave me almost unlimited access to all parts of her body, and her access to mine. No wonder pack wolves loved the ugly things so much.

My tongue danced with hers, wet and sweet and so very hot. I couldn't get enough of the feel of her mouth, needed to taste her in ways that were almost incomprehensible. Those red lips would be my downfall—could easily lead me straight to Heaven or Hell. I bit the plump bottom one gently, so very softly, just enough to hint at the level of desire I felt for her. She responded by pulling me closer and clawing at my back. The pleasure-pain of her nails in my skin caused goose bumps to break out along my arms and legs. I groaned in response and pressed my body harder against hers.

"Yes, I'll be on your balcony a little later." I trailed my lips over her jaw and bit the muscle on the side of her neck. She moaned and tilted her head in response as she sunk her teeth into my chest. Submissive and yet aggressive at the same time. The perfect mixture of sweet and saucy, my mate was. "We just need to finalize the plan details before I can come back up here."

Her hands slid down my back to grip my ass, pulling us together so she could grind her hip against my hard cock. My chest vibrated with the growl I tried to restrain as I fought the urge to sink my aching cock inside of her. She had me so hard, so painfully, excruciatingly in need of her. I was almost ready to beg her for a little release. Her hand, that irresistible mouth… anything. I'd had no idea my mating would come with such a raging case of blue balls.

Her lips moved to my neck. "Please don't keep me waiting."

"Never." I groaned as she sucked on my earlobe, her teeth making a small appearance at the end. "Fuck, you drive me wild, princess."

"I want you so much," she practically begged. The tone in her voice brought me to a new level of turned-on, dark and needy and completely desperate. I yanked her toward me with a growled curse, wedging my leg between hers and pulling her in tight so she could ride my thigh.

"Soon, sweet girl. Until then—" I tugged at our cloaks, pushing aside the fabric barrier between us. I caught a quick glimpse of her beautiful skin and soft curves before I pulled her into my embrace. Her naked breasts rested warm and soft against my chest, a sensation that quickly became my obsession. I wanted to lick them, suck the hardened tips into my mouth, and nuzzle the softness of her skin. Wanted to spend hours kneading the heavy flesh. But, at the moment, that would mean the possibility of others seeing those luscious tits, and I wasn't about to let that happen.

Turning her so my back blocked anyone coming up the stairs from seeing a single inch of all that pale skin, I lifted my leg higher against her pussy. The heat astounded me, making me moan as I imagined what all that soft, hot flesh would feel like wrapped around my needy cock. I slid one hand up around her hip to her breast, unable to stop myself, and pinched that coral-colored nipple between two fingers.

Kaija gasped and rocked her hips, her wetness spreading over my skin in a matter of seconds.

"Please, Lorenzo."

Hearing my name, my real name, fall from her lips on such a breathy sigh ignited my desire even further. Our kisses turned more heated, coming harder and faster as we rocked together. I wanted her to come so badly, needed it with every inch of my being. Teeth and tongue and flesh met as we tried to get closer, fought for more contact. Her pussy glided along the muscle of my thigh, teasing me with her heat, soaking me in her want.

"Now…please."

Her plea was my breaking point. I grabbed her by the back of her legs and lifted, ready to carry her to the nearest bed. Before I could take a single step in the direction of her suite, someone coughed from the top of the staircase. Kaija froze as I turned my head and glared at the intruder. Pup stood with his head slightly bowed, hand on the balustrade and a small smile on his face.

"They need you downstairs."

Kaija bit my collarbone and whined softly, a sound

that would forever haunt me as one filled with longing and disappointment. Something unacceptable to me as a man. I adjusted my grip on her legs to slide my fingers along her pussy from behind. She jumped and sighed as I teased her with the push-pull of my hand.

And then I focused on the interloper. "Leave us."

Kaija bit harder, and I took a backward step and rested my shoulders against the wall so I could press harder against her pussy.

"Yes…more." She moaned, lips against my collarbone, as I spread her open.

I slid one finger inside her, nearly howling as she squeezed around it. So tight, so hot. I pushed in a little farther, circling her entrance from within. She shivered in my arms and clenched down hard.

Another cough had me snarling. "Go away, Pup."

"If I don't come back with you, her father will come up here. And I'm pretty sure you don't want him to…uh…see this."

Kaija's walls fluttered around my finger, and I nearly whined at how close I knew she had to be. Two minutes. Two fucking minutes and I could have felt her shatter in my hand. Could have seen that same look of complete bliss cross her face as I'd made happen in our pine-tree den. But I didn't have two minutes unless I wanted Pup to hear her come in my arms. And that sound—the way her breath caught and she moaned almost without realization—was for my ears only.

Sliding my finger from her pussy, I pulled her body into mine and kissed the top of her head. The loss of her flesh against mine made me whimper, and by the look on her face, she felt the same.

"I'm so sorry we couldn't finish this, princess. I'll be back as soon as I can. I promise you." I set her down, straightening the fabric of her cloak to keep Pup from sneaking a peek.

She pressed her forehead to my chest as she panted. "I kind of hate you right now, you know that, right?"

The way her hands pulled me closer belied her words. I chuckled as I squeezed her one last time.

"I know, but I promise to make it up to you." A quick kiss to her head and I took a step away from her. Her cloak fell open, all that milky-white skin on display just for me. I groaned. "Princess."

She shrugged. "Sorry, it must have come unhooked somehow."

She smirked as she trailed her fingers over her breasts, tweaking a nipple along the way, before finally grasping the edges of the red fabric to hide herself once more.

"Tease," I whispered so Pup couldn't hear. She gave me a cheeky grin.

I took a deep breath and wished again for more time, more privacy, and more of my new mate. "Your brother Dante will be below your balcony, and Pup will be here in the hall. You're safe with them until I get back, okay?"

She nodded, her eyes locked on mine. "I'm not afraid."

I took a step away from her, never breaking our stare. "I have to go."

She stood stock-still, watching me leave.

"Hurry back."

ELEVEN

Gates

"SO IT'S DECIDED?" HALF Trac looked at each of us in turn. "Then if no one objects, let's retire for the evening. Tomorrow will be a big day."

He stood, his Cleaners following his lead. I stayed in my seat, glaring at a spot across the room, my heart in my throat and my bones aching. I hated the plan. I didn't doubt we could pull it off, but I hated it.

My mate would be used as bait. Against every argument I could possibly think of, the Breed and pack teams had agreed Kaija would be needed on the battlefield. The Feral Breed team would circle the escaping nomads, the Cleaners would assist us in destroying all but the leader, and the pack would be present as backup in case we needed assistance. But my mate would be the pretty little treat setting the trap. And I would not be the one making sure she stayed safely out of harm's way.

I hated that plan.

"You okay?" Sandman sat on the edge of the table across from me. I grunted in reply, unable and unwilling to communicate further.

Sandman sighed and leaned forward with his elbows on his

knees. "I know the fear within you, Gates. But put faith in us… We won't fail."

I stared hard at the man across from me. He'd lost his mate when he'd challenged his pack Alpha, so he understood the level of pain that would come to me should anything happen to Kaija. He knew how badly I would fight against any person or group that threatened her. Or at least he thought he did. Because no one in the Breed—not my denmates or my leaders or even my own brother—could understand the amount of evil lurking in the corners of my mind. For centuries, I'd been training, preparing myself for a battle I knew would one day come. And if this was it—if this was the moment I would unleash my inner animal fully to take out the danger to my mate—so be it. No one had any idea the level I would sink to protect her, or the lengths to which I would go to kill those who threatened us.

"You should go now, boy." I growled and sank farther into the chair, needing a few moments to myself to recapture the rage coursing through my body.

Sandman sighed and leaned forward with his elbows on his knees. "We won't fail. She'll return to camp safe and sound because we *will not* fail you, brother. There is nothing to fear."

My growl deepened, his ignorance inflaming my rage. I motioned for him to lean closer.

"When you see what you believe is fear within me, don't assume it's only for Kaija. Because as much as I'm afraid of the pain of losing her, it's not all that's burning inside of me. The fear the human side of me feels is for everything. It's for the very fabric of life as we know it." I grabbed Sandman by his T-shirt and yanked him toward me as I growled.

"If anything happens to her, anything at all, you had better hope she dies. If she dies, I die… It's that simple. But if she's injured? If they dare to take her away from me? I *will* seek vengeance. I'll bring a wrath down upon this planet until every possible participant in the offending party's life has been destroyed, without regard for collateral damage or bystanders. I'll spend the rest of my eternity looking for her if they manage to evade us again. I'll expose the secret; kill anyone who gets in my way. I'll annihilate our entire species to find my mate. There will be no stopping me. You think the worst thing to happen would be her death. I know the worst thing to happen would be if they took her. Because as long as she lives, as long as there's a bond between us and breath in my body, I will ravage the world to find her."

I stood, tossing him to the floor. "The nomads threatened to burn the camp down if we didn't comply with their demands. Cute threat… But they'd better be prepared. If they touch a single hair on Kaija's head, this Gatekeeper will set their entire world ablaze."

I SPENT AN HOUR after my talk with Sandman running through the woods on pack property. I needed to burn off the aggression pumping through my veins. I didn't want to scare Kaija or let her see me in such a state of distress. The idea of using her to lure the animals who'd already stolen her from her family once set my very soul on fire. No one would hurt her again. I knew she could defend herself if necessary, but I didn't want her to have to use those skills. It was my job as her mate, as her equal. I would protect her.

Missing her face and the softness of her body against mine, I ran toward the Alpha house. Dante stood under her balcony as I'd asked him to do.

"Go. Now."

He stiffened for a moment, obviously unaccustomed to being bossed around by anyone other than his father.

I closed my eyes and pulled out what little patience I had left. "Please."

With nothing more than a slight lip curl, he turned and raced for his cottage. I swung up onto Kaija's balcony quietly, not wanting to wake her had she fallen asleep. But her bed was empty when I peeked inside, the blankets turned down and the lighting in the room dimmed. The sound of water splashing caught my attention. Straight across from the screen I stood behind was the doorway to her en suite bathroom. Normally the door was closed, but tonight it stood open. I took a step to my left to double-check the room was clear and nearly fell over.

The bathroom was completely lit with candles. From my position on the balcony, I had a straight view to the tub at the far end of the space. The tub my mate was in…presumably naked…lifting her legs and rubbing a white cloth over all that gorgeous skin.

Have mercy, the woman is trying to kill me.

I let loose a growl, one I couldn't hold back. She paused for a second and smirked, but quickly continued her cleansing, pretending she didn't know I was there. But she knew. Of course she knew.

I pressed myself against the screen, desperate to be near her, wishing she would tell me to come in. I knew she wanted me with her, but I didn't want to invade her space without her permission. Not that watching her bathe wasn't invasive, though she had to have known I'd be here. She could have closed the door so as not to give me a show.

Unless she wanted me to see.

Her hands slid below the water, and she dropped her head back against the towel she'd placed at the back of the tub. A war erupted in my mind. Did I stay and watch? Stay and keep my eyes focused on the night sky, as hard as that might be? Leave the balcony and give her a chance to finish her ablutions?

The fact that a word I hadn't used in nearly a century had entered my mind in my moment of indecision made me realize how wrong it was to watch my young mate in such an exposed state. Suddenly feeling uncomfortable with my actions, I turned to look out over the forest below. But then she moaned.

"Oh, Gates. Mmmmmm, yes."

My eyes widened and my jaw fell as every ounce of blood I had rushed to my tortured cock. No way. There was no way she could be so cruel as to—

"Feels so good. Yes."

Fuck me, she *was* that cruel. She was getting off in the tub, knowing I was only feet away, knowing I could hear her. Or at least, I assumed she knew.

Just in case, I coughed to announce myself. "Are you okay in there, princess?"

I closed my eyes, wishing she would call for me, tell me to join her. That she would ask for my help or make the decision for me by demanding I leave. But she just giggled.

"I'm good, mate. Mmmm, yes. So good." Her breathing picked up as the sounds of splashing grew.

"Can you see me from out there? I wasn't sure if the candlelight would be enough."

I growled as I fought to keep my eyes closed. "I'm not looking, princess. I didn't want to…intrude."

The room fell silent, even her breathing seeming to soften as my words hung in the air. Tortuous. The lack of sound was absolutely tortuous. But then…

"Please look at me, Lorenzo."

I spun, my eyes meeting hers through the screen. Need, desire, want, lust, and affection looked back at me.

"I want you to watch me." Such emotion in those six words. Such hope and desire.

Adjusting myself and preparing for the hardest—no

pun intended—few moments of my life so far, I pressed my forehead to the screen and gave her a small nod. She smiled, all sweet and cute and completely fucking deadly before settling into the tub, bringing one foot up to rest against the rim. She made such a pretty picture—all red lips and pale skin against the pure-white of the ceramic fixtures. But dammit, I couldn't see enough. I nearly whimpered as her head rocked back and forth, her teeth biting into that full, red lip, wishing it was my own instead. She continued to moan and hum as she rocked against…something. Her hand? Yes, probably her hand. Fuck, I wanted it to be my hand. Wanted to feel how swollen she was from her need. Wanted to bury my fingers inside her and feel her tremble.

"Getting so close. This heat is killing me, Gates. I need release."

"Are you asking for my assistance?" My hands pressed into the woven surface of the screen as I waited for her response. Time slowed, every second lasting hours as I stood on the precipice of desire. But when she spoke, when she breathed a simple "Yes," the world restarted with a jolt.

The screen was no longer in my way. I had no memory of actually sliding it open, but that didn't matter. My feet moved of their own volition across the plush carpeting of her bedroom toward the light beckoning me. My mate was fully in her heat and she needed relief. That was my job, and thoughts of all I could do to sate her need consumed me. I would not leave her wanting.

"Gates."

"What do you need, sweet girl?"

Her eyes popped open. Bubbles obscured some of my view, though I'd seen almost everything before. The only part I'd not witnessed was the connection between her beautiful pussy and her hand. The way her fingers disappeared between her lips.

How the swollen flesh wrapped around her digits. She continued moving her hand as I watched, in and out, her thumb pressing against her clit in time with her thrusts. Beautiful, arousing, and sure to be the death of me.

She opened her legs a little farther as her fingers increased their speed. "You came."

I huffed a laugh. "Not yet."

Her returning smirk was positively wicked. "Me neither. Think you can help me out with that?"

I hovered over the tub, leaning down to place a small kiss on her wet lips. "We'll be breaking a few rules."

She moaned and moved her hand faster, biting her lip again. "I don't care about the rules. I just want to be with you."

I nearly groaned in relief. "As you wish."

I slid my arms under her body and yanked her up into my hold. She squeaked but didn't offer a complaint, just leaned her head against my chest as I carried her out of the candlelit room. Drowning in the scent of her need, I walked her to her bed and placed her gently on top of the blanket.

"Gates," she whispered as her nails dug into my shoulders. "Please."

"I can't have you yet, princess." I picked up her leg and rested her foot on my shoulder as I ran my tongue along the curve of her knee. "If we start our bonding, I won't want to stop, and we're not free from the threat yet. But I know you're in heat. I can smell it on you. I can practically feel your frustration." I knelt at the side of her bed, holding eye contact as I pulled her ass to the very edge and draped her legs over my shoulders. "Let me help you."

A single nod was the only permission I needed before I dove in. My lips and tongue made contact with her soft, pink flesh as I groaned and fought the urge to just take her. Her pussy tasted as perfect as I'd imagined, and I made sure to lick every inch in my quest to please her. Her gasps taught me what she liked, her moans what she loved. And when she arched off the mattress and fisted her hands in my hair, I knew I'd learned exactly how to make her come. I tongued her clit hard and fast, rubbing my teeth along the hood and holding her lips open for my assault. She rocked against my face, alternating moans and pants as I savored her.

When she lifted her ass off the bed, pressing herself against my tongue, I took her hint for more. Without warning, I slid two fingers inside her. I curled them, searching for the spot that would drive her crazy. I pumped them in and out, pressing harder with each swipe, pushing deeper and deeper as I teased and stroked inside. And then I found it. Her feet dug into my shoulders when I slid my fingers over the fleshy spot, and her moan grew loud and solid. I hoped her packmates guarding outside could hear it. I hoped they would know her mate, the only man who would ever get this close to her pussy again, was sating her. I hoped they heard and knew not to come near her.

She tried to bring her legs together as her walls fluttered around my fingers, but I didn't let her. I wedged my shoulders between her knees and held her open, plunging and curling and sucking and licking until her entire body shivered and she keened with the force of her upcoming orgasm.

"Gates…Gates…Ga-Lorenzo."

Her pussy squeezed my hand, tight and hot and wet, just as I'd imagined it would. I craved it, needed to feel it wrapped around my cock, couldn't wait to sink into her. I would happily die in her arms with my cock in her pussy, but not before I'd felt her come all around me the way she was coming around my fingers. Fuck, the pressure was astounding, sucking my hand inside and making my balls crawl up into my body with a need so powerful, I nearly came.

Panting, groaning, and growling, I continued to play with

her as she shuddered through her release. When she relaxed back into the mattress, I softened my touch but didn't stop, making sure she held on to every ounce of pleasure possible until she finally pulled her legs in and rolled away from me.

"Tender, princess?" I pressed my lips to the side of her thigh and rested my head on her hip.

"Goodness, I needed that."

I chuckled. "Glad I could be of service."

"Hmmm." She shifted up the bed, reaching for me as she went. "Lay with me."

"I don't think that's such a good idea."

Her pout, while endearing, broke my heart a little. I didn't want to turn her down, but if I didn't find some relief of my own soon, I was going to explode.

"You get some rest." I pulled the covers over her body and placed a kiss on her forehead. She opened her eyes just a smidge, then promptly closed them again.

"I'm going to have a lot to make up for next time I drag you into my closet."

I laughed as I strode toward the balcony door, my cock so hard it hurt. "I'll hold you to that."

She sighed as I stepped out onto the balcony. With a quick glance around, I vaulted over the railing and landed soundlessly on the grass below. Two minutes. It was all I needed. The woman had me in a constant haze of lust. Even with all the kissing and grinding and rutting we were doing, I was still sporting a hard-on ninety percent of the time.

"You okay there, boss?"

I spun, growling at Sandman as he leaned against the tree at the corner of the house. "What are you doing here?"

He shrugged. "Listening to you do a bang-up job of relieving your mate's heat needs."

I growled. What I did or did not do with my mate was

none of—

"Easy, man. I'm not trying to overstep. I saw when you stepped inside and thought I'd better stay close in case you got…distracted. And now I'm wondering if you would perhaps need a few minutes alone. I can keep an eye on her door so you can take care of"—he waved a hand at hip level—"business."

If I'd been a twelve-year-old boy, I might have blushed. But I wasn't. I was a man with needs who'd just spent ten minutes with his face buried in a pussy he had yet to have full access to. Something had to give.

"Five minutes, tops." My voice nearly cracked on the last word, but Sandman either didn't notice or chose to ignore it. Good man.

"No one will get past me, brother. I *will* keep her safe."

"Thanks." I ran off into the woods, pulling open the fly of my jeans as I went. I had barely made it to the tree line when I wrapped my fingers around myself and began to pump. I used the hand I'd had buried in Kaija's pussy only minutes before, the thought making it seem hotter and softer than usual. Up and down I teased as I hurried to what I hoped would be a spot private enough for a quick wank.

When I finally reached the side of a giant pine tree, the branches fallen in a way to shield me, I pulled my cock the rest of the way out and thrust into my hand with force. Fuck, I could still smell Kaija on me. Spicy and sweet, the scent made my arousal burn hotter. I licked my lips and threw my head back as my hand slid up and down my length, swiping my thumb around the tip every few strokes. Pictures of my mate in the throes of her orgasms flashed through my mind. The way she would toss her head back and her mouth would fall open, how she would squeeze her eyes shut and gasp as the first flutters wracked her body. The flush that would settle over her chest and face as the intensity swelled and she rode out every last second of her orgasm. Beautiful…delectable…

"Mine."

I came with a jolt, my entire body locking down with the pleasure of my release. Soon. I would come inside her soon, and then I would get to feel all that soft heat wrapped around my cock instead of my own hand.

With little regard to the mess I'd made, I hurried back toward the house, tucking my now-softened cock in my pants and zipping as I ran. Shadow stood sentry as I'd left him, looking off toward the east.

"I'll stay down here tonight," he said before I even reached him.

"I've got the balcony."

"Yes, but your mate sounds to be in the worst hours of her heat." He turned to meet my gaze, far-off look in his eyes. "I met my Margaret in late fall and was forced to wait until summer for our Klunzad time. That winter, when she went into heat, she would cry and shake from the pain. The only thing that seemed to help her was my touch, so I would sneak into her room and wrap myself around her to help her sleep. Perhaps your new mate would find the same relief if you two shared skin-on-skin contact this evening, old friend."

Kaija moaned as Sandman spoke, drawing my attention to her door. It was not a moan of pleasure, but one of pain.

"Hurry. Your mate needs you." Sandman nodded toward the balcony, and then took a step away, nearly disappearing into the shadows of the house. "I'll stand guard. I won't let you down."

Swallowing the lump that had formed in my throat, I watched my friend and Breed brother as he settled in to protect my mate. He would stand guard all night, I knew. He would make sure I never had to live through the hell he had when he lost his mate.

"Thank you, brother."

"Cherish her. Fight for her. Never trust the pack."

With a nod, I jumped onto the balcony. The wind had picked up, bringing with it the cool air off the lake. Fall was short in this part of the country. Soon, winter would come. A time for mating and breeding and huddling up in a warm place together. Where that place would be was not my decision to make; it was Kaija's. I would respect it because that was our custom, but Sandman's words sent my mind spiraling into a sea of doubt.

Because when the wind blew cold and the smell of the coming winter danced on the breeze, when I dreamed of a place safe and warm to hole up with my mate, that place was not on Valkoisus land. And I somehow knew Kaija would not want to leave.

Hearing my mate in discomfort, I hurried to open the screen. Kaija tossed and turned in her bed. Her skin was flushed and her legs were twisted in the sheets as if she'd been writhing since the moment I left her.

Once I reached her side, I brushed a lock of hair off her face and leaned down to kiss her. "Kaija? Are you okay?"

She whimpered and curled into a ball. "It hurts, Gates. It's never hurt like this before."

"I know, princess. I think I can help you. Do you want me to try?"

She nodded against the pillow. "Please."

I tossed her blanket to the floor and yanked the sheet from under her. I kept my eyes locked with hers as I removed my cut, T-shirt, and jeans. She didn't say a word, just watched me undress with nothing more than a sigh.

"If I didn't know better, I'd say my body doesn't entice you."

She shook her head. "Of course it entices me, but I can't have you. And yet you stand there before me naked. Why are you teasing me so?"

I lifted her and sat her on the edge of the bed. Before she could protest, I pulled the silk nightdress over her head, relieved to see her naked underneath.

"I'm not teasing you, princess. Skin-to-skin contact will help ease your pain, so we must be naked."

"If you get into this bed with me naked, there's no way we won't have sex."

I pulled the sheet out of the way. "We won't have sex. I can control myself."

"But what if I can't?"

"Then we'll say screw pack laws and do whatever it takes to make the pain go away." I lay down on the mattress. "C'mere."

With a tug, I pulled her down on top of me. I wrapped my legs around hers and pulled her into my arms even as her head came to rest on my chest. Once she seemed comfortable, I yanked the sheet over us before retuning my hands and arms to cover her back. Full contact from toes to nose.

"That feels better already," she mumbled.

I chuckled and held her tight, loving the way she fit against me. "Get some sleep, princess. Tomorrow is a busy day."

She sighed and snuggled closer before her breathing evened out. The weight of her against me made my heart practically sing. My mate, in my arms with nothing between us, was practically a dream come true. But with the joy came the fear, and with the fear came the rage. Kaija would meet the nomads in the morning. Alone. Or as close to alone as one could be with a full pack and a team of Feral Breed brothers there to make sure nothing went wrong. Yet I would not be close. I would be on the opposite hillside, watching from above.

Waiting to unleash the hell within me should something go wrong.

So as my mate slept in my arms, I stared at the ceiling

and began planning all the ways I would eviscerate her former captors if they somehow succeeded in their plans.

TWELVE

THE WIND BLEW IN from the north, bringing with it the smell of the lake. It comforted me with its familiarity. I stood in the center of a clearing near an old smelter long ago abandoned, the required location for the exchange as set by the men who'd taken me the first time. Sandman stood slightly behind and to my left. The figurehead of the Feral Breed crew. The man charged with protecting me should things go wrong.

I hoped for everyone's sake things didn't go wrong.

I watched as the wind stirred the pine trees, causing a dance of green needles on a multihued brown stage. Beautiful and powerful, this land had once been a vibrant and strong provider of copper for the world. Now, the mines sat empty, the men and women who'd worked in them moved on to other places. Yet we Valkoisus shifters stayed. Our pack had made a home in these woods for hundreds of years, and we would be here for hundreds of years to come. We were strong, we were able, and we would not be torn asunder by the likes of a group of nomads with an Omega obsession.

When I'd awoken that morning, Gates had set my mind at ease with sweet words and even sweeter kisses. But once he'd left to prepare for the fake exchange, my nerves had taken over. I'd worried and fretted over every detail. But then Half Trac came to see me. He spoke at length with me about my power as an Omega, teaching me in moments things I hadn't learned in my decades of life.

There were many mysteries of the Omegas, many secrets as well. But one thing was for sure and well known—there was an innate power growing within us from the moment of our birth. And there were many shifters who would lie, cheat, steal, and kill to have access to that power, even if they didn't know how to access it. That threat was the reason why my father had refused to allow my presence at a Gathering. It was why I'd been kept secluded from the outside shifter world. And it was why I had confidence we would all make it through this day alive.

Playing Half Trac's words over in my head, I closed my eyes and dug deep into what I thought of as my wolf spirit. I searched for the thread of connection I felt to my mate. Gates was not allowed near the clearing during the exchange, but he wasn't far. I knew he wouldn't be. He would never allow great distance between us, especially not when I was in danger, just as I would never allow him to go into a battle alone. We were one—one heart, one soul, one powerful unit even before our official bonding. But today I would have to act alone.

I breathed deep, centering myself in the moment and concentrating on the link to Gates. The itch of a shift started at my head and fell over me, all the way down to my toes. It was almost time. Soon, the nomads would arrive. Soon, I would fully utilize my Omeganess for the first time.

Soon, I would help Half Trac and his Cleaners capture any nomad who threatened my mate, my pack, my Omega sisters, or me.

As the first scent of the nomads reached me, I opened my

eyes and prepared myself for what I knew was to happen. They would come; they would take me; the Feral Breed team would save me.

Or so they thought.

Half Trac had made sure I understood the plan that was explained to the teams, the one where the Breed team would rescue me followed by a contingent of pack wolves to eliminate the nomads and capture the leader. It had been a good plan, one everyone agreed to. But in our meeting, Half Trac altered almost every detail in a secret plan only he and I would know about. For his benefit as well as to keep my Gates from danger. My team was good, my pack and the Breed strong, but they would not be saving me today. My mission was clear—let the nomads take me, wait for the Cleaners, open my Omega power to them so they could capture—not kill—all the nomads.

The pack would not need to rescue me.

The Feral Breed would not need to rescue me.

My mate would not need to rescue me.

The power of the Omega that lurked within would rescue me.

It was time for the princess of the Valkoisus pack to earn her crown.

Gates

I FELT THE FIRST tug on my mating bond as I waited on a hillside looking over the clearing where Kaija stood. I watched, waiting for a sign or a signal, something to tell me what was happening to her that caused the twinge in my heart. But nothing happened. She remained motionless, a brilliant red statue standing in a forest of green.

The tug increased as I noticed the wolves coming over the hill opposite me. Just as we'd expected, they'd come in from the west. Six wolves and three men walked through the woods toward my mate, one of them obviously Magnus. Even from where I sat, hidden hundreds of yards away, I could see they'd not been easy on him. Battered and bloody, he stumbled his way down the hill and toward Sandman, who stood with Kaija.

I'd known from the time the plan had been laid out that these would be the hardest five minutes of my life. I was forced to stay back with a team of pack wolves and allow the nomads to come close to my mate, to take possession of her, to begin their trek back the way they'd come. The time would be a true test of my control, and I worried I would not survive it.

As the nomads walked into the clearing, the tug on my mate bond increased. Something was wrong. I could almost taste it on the brisk wind blowing in from the lake. Something dark and dank was coming my way, bringing blood and grief with it.

Something like death danced on the wind.

Kaija

"YOU KNOW, PRINCESS. YOU get prettier and prettier every time I see you."

The leader of the nomads walked through the tree line and into the clearing. A second shifter in human form, the short one who'd taken such perverse joy in torturing my sister, dragged Magnus along with him. The wolves came next. Six of them, all growling and snarling as they padded cautiously through the trees. I watched silently, unafraid. The plan would work. The Cleaners would come. There could be no doubt on my part.

"Yeah, yeah, she's a looker. Let's get this over with." Sandman placed his hand on my lower back. I stumbled forward, acting as if he'd shoved me, as was part of the plan. I was not supposed to appear willing. No matter how anxious I was to be alone with the nomads so we could get this over with.

"Easy on the merchandise, man." The leader stepped

forward and grabbed my arm, dragging me all the way behind the line of wolf defenders he'd brought. "My boss wouldn't be too happy if we broke his new toy before he got his chance to play with her."

He nodded toward his partner, and the man shoved Magnus across the gap to where I'd stood only moments before. I met Sandman's eyes as he helped Magnus stay on his feet. Fear. As strong as he was and as brave as I knew him to be, Sandman was afraid for me. Or maybe afraid for everyone should something happen to me. I wasn't dumb—my mate would become a ball of rage should any harm befall me. And I knew, from my own observations as well as my conversation with Half Trac, Gates was not a man to be messed with even in his best of moods.

The fates truly had chosen our pairing well, but I wasn't willing to risk his life for mine when there were other, safer options. Half Trac would keep my mate as calm as possible while I helped the Cleaners capture our enemies. We just needed to get to a place where Gates couldn't see what I was about to do.

"We'll just be on our way now." The leader tugged me up the hill, moving fast as his wolves closed in behind us to guard our retreat. "I'll let my boss know how cooperative the so-called protectors of the species were. I'm sure it'll give him a good laugh."

"Hey, nomad," Sandman hollered from behind us. I glanced over my shoulder as the leader turned. There was no fear left, no worry or doubt. The man looking at us was all confidence and bravado, ready to fight and sure he'd win. "I'll be seeing you soon."

The leader squeezed my arm and yanked me up and over the hill until I could no longer see the clearing behind me. A few more minutes. The Cleaners would come once there was enough distance between the Breed contingent and us. Just a little more time.

Thirty yards down the hill, a giant roar sounded through the forest, sending the birds to the air and the small animals scurrying. My heart leapt in my chest as all the things that could go wrong slammed into my thoughts: death, injuries, destruction, and annihilation. Gates must have seen the Breed not respond as the original plan had been laid out. He must have assumed they were letting the men take me. My mate didn't know the Cleaners would help me fight the nomads. He didn't know I was taking on the risk to keep him out of the fight.

My mate was coming for me...and there was a very real possibility that he would die while trying to save me.

Gates

THE NOMAD HAD HIS hand on my mate. I waited and watched from my perch, unable to hear the words being spoken. But I didn't need to—the fucker was touching my mate. He would die for that alone.

Movement. The nomad team was leaving, dragging Kaija with them. I watched them crest the hill and disappear down the other side, my heart racing the entire time.

"What are they doing?" Rex asked, standing at my side. He hadn't liked being sidelined any more than I had. He wasn't even supposed to be this close, but he'd barged onto the overlook to watch over his sister.

"I have no fucking clue."

The Feral Breed team was supposed to move in as soon as the nomads crested the hill, surround them, and get Kaija back before killing all but the leader. Yet I saw no movement on our side. Even Sandman, who'd sworn to me that he would not let anything happen to my mate, stood in the clearing, doing nothing more than arguing with Half Trac. A certain cock to

Sandman's head had me looking closer, and my blood turned to ice as I saw the telltale signs of a forced Alpha order.

Sandman wasn't just arguing…he was trying to fight off Half Trac's demand to stay put. Glancing at the rest of my brothers, I saw the same things. Heads cocked, muscles straining, faces twisted into grimaces. Meanwhile Half Trac stood in the middle, doing nothing but watching my mate be taken from me.

They were going to let her go, and the only hope I had from my Breed leadership was that those fucking Cleaners could get to her. Three shifters against eight with my little mate caught in the crossfire.

"Half Trac lied." Rex's voice cut through the silence. The entire pack team froze for a beat as that knowledge sank in. Kaija was in trouble, and my brothers, who'd been assigned to help her, had been handicapped by their supposed leader.

The boiling sensation of my rage bubbled up from the bottom of my gut, overpowering all sense of reason. I would kill them all. Every last shifter in these woods would die in my battle to get Kaija back. Fuck the pack, fuck the Breed, fuck the world. My mate was in danger.

I roared as my body shifted into my lupine form, muscles and bones twisting in less than a second. I was running from the first impact of paw on dirt. I raced down the hill toward my traitorous leader. Panting, I pumped my legs harder than ever before. I sped through trees and jumped over rocky outcroppings on my way to the clearing. On my way to destroy the world around me and get my mate back.

"Lorenzo Martinez de Caballero, you shall bow to my will."

My legs locked, causing me to tumble ass over end through the dirt. I whimpered as I hit a large rock half buried in the ground. The telltale snap of a bone breaking the only sound recognizable over my own heart racing.

"Gatekeeper." Half Trac knelt beside me, his eyes glowing and his hand held over my head. I wanted to tell him to fuck off, to fight my way up and get to my mate, but I couldn't move. Something held me in place on the ground, completely at the mercy of those around me. "Shift back, now."

I squealed as his words forced my body to shift to human form. Painfully, slowly, bringing back vivid images of those first few shifts I'd experienced as a child. Shifting was a natural inclination for us Borzohn, or birthed shifters, but still one that took time to learn and perfect. Those first few shifts had been brutal, and this one was no better. Especially with what I had to assume was a broken arm. Half Trac watched with those glowing eyes, waiting until I was fully human before pulling his hand away.

"I will not hurt you, and your mate will be fine. She is a powerful Omega, especially for one so young. Her power will protect her."

"Need…my mate."

Half Trac chuckled and shook his head as I fought the hold he had over me. "The nomads cannot access her power, young one. They are useless—unpacked, undisciplined, and unwilling to bend to a higher power. No, they are of no concern to me. Kaija's power as an Omega will protect her, as will my Cleaners. I could not risk the death of those nomads, not when we still don't know who their supposed leader is. I am more concerned about finding out what they know than what they've done, and that means we can't kill them. We need answers first."

I struggled harder, my heart racing faster as I felt the weakening of my bond to Kaija. She was moving away from me.

"Let me up!"

"Settle, please. I would not allow anything to happen to your mate. Her pack and yours will soon follow the nomads to keep them corralled in the valley. My Cleaners will apprehend the men while your brothers make sure she is returned to you alive and well."

Before I could speak again, the tug on my mating bond turned to a feeling of energy and solidness, blanketing me in a sense of power I'd never experienced. It fueled me and gave me the strength to pull myself from Half Trac's hold. I rolled and jumped to my feet, shaking off the odd sensation of whatever power Half Trac had put over me. My Breed brothers around me followed suit, each breaking through the hold Half Trac had put over us. I didn't know what had given us the strength to overthrow such a powerful Alpha, but I had a feeling it had something to do with Kaija.

My brothers approached, glares and growls directed at Half Trac who stood motionless and obviously shocked. I wanted to kill the lying bastard for what he'd done, for the risk he'd put Kaija in, but I didn't have the time. My mate needed me, and I couldn't fail her.

"You lied to me and my Breed brothers, you broke the covenants of our trust, and you put Kaija in danger. Be gone when I get back, or your blood will flow the same as those nomads who stupidly thought they could lay their hands on my mate."

Without a backward glance, I raced through the trees and over the hill. Running for my life. Running for my mate. Power infused my body and made me run faster than ever before. The world was a blur around me, my feet never missing purchase as I ran through the trees.

Sandman and Pup ran a few feet behind me, only catching up when we crested a particularly steep hill on our way to block the nomads.

"You ready for this?" Sandman pushed off from a rocky outcropping and landed with a slide a few feet in front of me.

"More than." I swung around a tree and under branches, the world hurtling past me in a blur of green and brown.

"Get your mate, brother. We've got your back. The others are on their way to circle around just in case the fuckers get away from us."

With that, Sandman and Pup swung out to encircle the valley where the nomads were. I paid them no mind, though. My eyes found the red of my mate's cloak among the earth tones of the forest and refused to look away as I raced to protect the only thing I'd ever truly needed in my life.

THIRTEEN

"WHAT THE HELL WAS that?" The leader of the nomads spun and stumbled. Gates' roar had scared him, as well it should have.

Knowing my time was limited, I focused on the pull to my mate. Warm and strong, the thread to him glowed bright red in my mind. I held on to it, focused completely on the gentle hum it provided me. I concentrated on that thread, willing my Omega strength into the line connecting us. If Gates was coming, he would need my help. The Omega power I was supposed to use to strengthen the Cleaners in their efforts to capture the nomads would have to be shared between us. Because there was no way I was letting my mate take on eight nomad shifters alone.

"Let's get the fuck out of here." Lanie's tormentor grabbed my arm and pushed me forward. I stumbled but held myself upright even as I continued to focus on that red thread. My body shook as the bond solidified, imbued with all the strength I could muster. My actions negated the new plan Half Trac had designed, but I could not risk Gates. The Cleaners would need to fight for themselves; I needed to give my strength to my mate.

"What the hell is wrong with her?"

My head fell back as the power of the Omega flowed through me, over me, within me. This was the gift of a mated Omega—a deadly and aggressive energy to share with those who needed protecting. Shifter lore said our power was something virtual, something that merely made our pack bonds stronger. The lore was a fallacy. Omega power was a physical thing we could grab and use when needed. It could make our pack bonds more powerful because of the unconscious desire of shifters to congregate near all that power. But it could also be shared with our fellow shifters to give them physical strength in a time of war. Only an Omega could wield it. Only an Omega could use it to save herself and her pack.

And this Omega was going to share her power with her mate to keep him safe in battle.

Whether the mating was "pack official" or not.

Members of the Breed appeared from the tree line surrounding us, encircling the nomad group and moving closer like a fishing net on a retrieval.

"You're done here, man." Sandman stalked closer, his eyes on the nomad who held me.

"If you come closer, I'll kill her."

Sandman laughed, dark and filled with an evil timbre I'd never heard from him. "You do that, and you'll be wishing for death before her body even hits the ground. The Gatekeeper is coming. Executioner for the Feral Breed, brother to the Beast, and mated to the woman you hold against her will. You've fucked up, friend."

The arms of the nomad no longer held me. I fell forward at the loss of support. A roar sounded as I fell to my knees, and I knew things were about to get ugly.

My Gates had arrived.

Gates

I RACED AROUND A copse of trees in time to see Kaija fall to the ground. The roar I released was enough to have the shifter who'd dared to lay his hands on her look my way. His jaw fell open as he stumbled backward into the leader of the nomads.

"Kaija!" I leapt over a fallen tree trunk as I headed toward the men I knew as dangerous to my mate. Kaija hurried to her feet, but before I could reach her, a shifter in wolf form slammed into me from the side. I curled and rolled, hopping to my feet to face the fucker in human form.

He growled and curled his lip as another wolf joined him. The two stalked closer, heads down and napes bristled. Even as I watched them, I kept Kaija in my peripheral vision. I would not lose sight of her again. The longer these two kept me away from my mate, the more painful their deaths would be.

I noticed Rex arrive and move toward his sister, which was good. He would help me keep her safe. I trusted him as I trusted my Feral Breed brothers. Refocusing on the assholes standing between Kaija and me, I adjusted my stance and smirked.

"You two gonna to do something here, or are we just going to dance all day?"

Lefty growled and jumped at me. I hunched down and struck from below, ripping open his abdomen with my claws. Righty hit me as I rolled onto my back. Jaws snapping and slobber flying, he snapped and barked and did his best to get ahold of my throat. But I was smarter, better trained, and full of a strength the likes of which I'd never experienced. I threw him off me with a swipe of my arm and followed him as he rolled away. Kaija and Rex fighting against the shorter man caught my attention, giving Righty enough of an opportunity to come at me again. We continued this way for three more rounds, me shoving him off at every attack but losing focus as I watched my mate spin and kick and punch. Finally, when I was pinned under the beast yet again, I heard her voice reach me through all his growling.

"For the love of the gods, Lorenzo. Just kill the man."

I grinned even as I struggled to pull my arm free from his jaws. "Yes, dear."

With more strength than I knew I had, I pulled my legs up and kicked the furry little fuck off me and across the clearing. Unfortunately, his teeth took a good chunk of my bicep with him. Bleeding and cursing the pain, I struggled to my feet and hurried toward my mate. Rex had the short fucker on the ground, while Shadow and Pup had made it through the melee to surround Kaija. There looked to be only three nomad wolves left alive, one of whom was trying to circle Sandman as he subtly led the creature away from my mate.

"You know, son," Sandman said to the wolf. "You really picked the wrong day to screw with us. I'm pretty sure I've never felt more ready for a fight than I do right now."

The wolf growled as Sandman smirked. The sound of a gun being fired interrupted the moment and made my heart nearly stop. Rex lay on the ground, clutching his knee as he rolled around in obvious agony. I raced toward Kaija's side as the wolf jumped at a distracted Sandman, knocking him to the ground. Pup leapt into the fight, leaving only one nomad for me to battle.

A short motherfucker with a gun trained on my mate.

I slid to a stop a few feet in front of Kaija, looking the nomad right in the eye.

"You really don't want to point that thing at her."

He huffed a laugh. "Either she comes with me, or she dies. You pick, Gatekeeper."

I raised my arms to the side and shook my head. "You'll

have to get through me to touch her."

Nomad's smile turned wicked and he aimed the gun over my shoulder. "Fastest way to take you down is to kill her."

I yelled and jumped as he fired. A streak of red slammed into his side and knocked him to the ground at the same time my claws raked into his flesh. The bullet hit me in the side of my abdomen as I tore through his throat, blood pouring from each of us to redden the ground.

"Gates!"

Kaija appeared over me before I'd even stopped sliding across the gravel. I wrapped my uninjured arm around her and tried to push her behind me, clinging to my midsection with the other. I knew I'd gotten the son of a bitch, but I had no idea if he was dead or not. I needed her protected. But Kaija struggled against my hold, and between my damaged arm and the pain radiating from where I'd been shot, I was having a hard time holding her.

"Kaija, get back." I pushed again, struggling to my knees to shield her. Kaija finally pressed her front to my back and wrapped one arm around my neck.

"Damn it, stop." Kaija's voice yelling in my ear made me freeze. My body shook as I panted, pain and adrenaline drastically affecting my focus. "Gates, look." Kaija pointed to where the short shifter now lay in a pile of broken bones and spilled blood. I'd done it... I'd protected my mate. I nearly sagged in relief until a new shadow passed over us. A man I recognized as one of Half Trac's Cleaners stood over the fallen shifter, gun in hand and pointed our way.

"It wasn't supposed to be like this."

FOURTEEN

Kaija

"IT WASN'T SUPPOSED TO be like this."

I sighed with relief even as the hulking Cleaner pointed the gun at us.

"It's okay." I grasped Gates' shoulder and looked over him to the Cleaner. "I'm in no danger from my mate."

The Cleaner stared at Gates for a long moment, and then tucked the gun into the holster under his arm.

"My apologies, Gatekeeper." The Cleaner grabbed the short shifter off the ground and threw him over his shoulder. "Blaze's orders were very clear. Protect the Omega no matter who the threat appeared to be. I know you're her mate, but I couldn't take the risk."

"I thought you were here with Half Trac?" Gates glanced at me before pulling me around into his lap. Blood poured from the bicep of the arm holding his midsection, and I had a feeling there would be more blood coming from that wound. My brave mate had taken quite a lot of damage for me.

The Cleaner snorted. "That little fucker has a tendency to think he's bigger than he is. Yes, we were sent with Half Trac to assist in the mission, but Blaze's orders outrank all others. Half

Trac wanted to change the plan to have us capture the nomads instead of killing them, but Blaze was clear. Protect the Omega, no matter what." He looked at me and smiled. "I'm sorry my associate was crass with you the other day; he'll be dealt with after we report back to Blaze on the situation. Please know you were never in any danger here today. Whether you shared your Omega power with us or not, we were prepared to kill for you."

I nodded but quickly glanced down when something warm and wet slid over my leg.

"Gates…you're bleeding."

Gates pulled me closer even as he shook his head. "I'm fine."

"You're not fine. You're bleeding all over me." I stood and pulled off my cloak, revealing the jeans and long-sleeved shirt I'd worn underneath. Just in case. "Lie down, you can use this as a pillow until we can carry you out of here."

"I said I was fine." Gates pushed himself up as if to stand, but the Cleaner put a heavy hand on his shoulder and gave him a stern look.

"The Omega said stay down. I suggest you take her directive."

I fought a smile as Gates grumbled. "Are the other Cleaners nearby?"

The man still gripping Gates' shoulder whistled, and his two teammates walked into the clearing from where they'd hidden. They wore camouflage and had their faces painted to better blend in to the landscape, which probably why I hadn't noticed them earlier.

"We've got two men down who need more medical attention than the medic can provide." The Cleaner addressed his team as Shadow, Pup, and Sandman joined our group. "I've got the Omega. Diesel, you take dark and cranky. Butz can grab Cappers."

"Cappers?" I asked.

The Cleaner smiled at me. "Your brother got kneecapped. That shit hurts and doesn't always heal right, but he did it fighting to save you. That earned our respect, and therefore he gets an honorary road name."

Gates groaned as Diesel lifted him into a fireman's hold. I rushed over, my mouth falling open as I saw the amount of blood coming from the wound on his side. Shifters may have extraordinary healing powers, but losing blood was our weakness. No blood, no healing. No Gates.

"We need to hurry."

SMOKE. IT TEASED MY senses, the acrid odor pulling me from sleep. I buried my face in my pillow, which smelled oddly of Gates. It didn't matter how or why, I suddenly needed to immerse myself in him. Something dark and dangerous pulled me from my memories, but I blocked it as best I could. I wanted to sleep. I wanted to roll in Gates' scent and spend the next two days unconscious. I curled into a ball and pulled the covers over my head to trap the spicy smell against my skin.

"I was wondering if you were ever going to wake up."

My eyes popped open, looking across the naked expanse of Gates' chest I was apparently resting on. When I lifted the edge of the quilt I'd covered myself with, I met the amused gaze of my mother. "How long have I been asleep?"

She sat in a slipper chair near the entrance to my bedroom with her iridescent maroon cloak fanned around her. Perfect, pristine, and yet paler than I'd ever seen her. I knew the last few days had been hard on her; they'd been hard on all of us. But I hadn't expected to see her so obviously…upset.

"Nearly a whole day. The Feral Breed medic said you would be fine, but I will admit I was beginning to worry. And your poor mate was practically in a panic when he couldn't wake you."

"Gates was awake?" I pushed up onto one arm and inspected my sleeping mate. His color looked good, and he didn't appear to be bleeding anymore. And yet he slept.

"Yes, but not for very long. He's still a little weak from the blood loss and needs his rest." She smiled softly at the man lying beside me. "He's a good man, very protective of you."

"I know." I took a deep breath and stared at the ceiling, reliving the day before in my mind. "He's killed a lot of people. And I told him to kill a nomad during the fight."

"Yes, I know."

When I looked at her, my mother had her head tilted and a calm expression on her face. No sign of revulsion or surprise. I sat up, wrapping the blanket around my naked shoulders and pulling my knees to my chest.

"I never thought I would be okay with murder."

Mother crossed the room to sit on the edge of the bed and pulled me into her side. "No, I wouldn't have thought you would. But our world is dangerous, daughter. Especially for you. When I think of what those men intended…"

She looked toward the door and sniffed. After a few seconds, she turned and met my eyes. "The gods only know what their true intentions were, but I can't imagine any of them being good. Their deaths should not rest on your conscience."

I took a deep breath as my eyes burned with the tears I fought.

"You don't think less of him because of what he did? Or of me because I wanted that man dead?"

"Never, and not just because you are my beloved daughter and Gates your fated mate. You were taken, stolen in the night by a bunch of cowards who tried to set up a fight between our chosen protectors and our pack by making us trade their leader for you. They gave us no choice and showed no remorse for their actions. If the Breed hadn't killed those men, I don't know if you would be sitting here right now." She wiped tears from her cheeks and met my eyes, her gaze unwavering. "I will forever be grateful to fate for bringing us your mate and his brothers of the Feral Breed at such an important time. As strong as we are, our pack is not trained to fight the way those men are. They are our defenders, not something to be feared or to look upon with disdain. They are a true blessing to us. And they did nothing wrong."

I glanced at Gates as he rolled to his side, wrapping his upper body around me. He craved my touch even in his sleep, which made me smile.

My mother reached over and brushed Gates' hair off his forehead. "Killer or no, the man cares for you and will keep you happy and safe. I can ask for nothing more than that."

I smiled a watery smile. "I'm almost sad Gates is leaving the Breed, though I have to admit the idea of him joining our pack is not a bad one."

"What do you mean? Why would he leave the Breed?"

"Because he's my mate. I don't want to leave here, and it's my right to make that choice for us."

She stood, her face dark with concern. "Kaija, that man is not meant for pack life. He will never be happy here."

My gut clenched as she voiced the fear that had been percolating in the back of my mind since the first moment we met. "Perhaps he will adjust."

"There is no adjusting for men like him. The Feral Breed is more than a motorcycle club. It's a brotherhood. Those men live together, fight together, and rely on one another to stay alive. And your Gates has been a member for almost two hundred years. He will not *adjust.*"

I swallowed hard and refused to meet her eyes. "You can't know that."

"Oh, daughter. You have so much to learn." She pulled my hair back from where it hung in my face. "I want you happy and safe, mated to a man who will make you smile and help hold you up when you need it. But life with a partner is not easy. There are sacrifices and compromises that must be made, on both sides, even with fate helping you along the way. You would be wise to remember that."

I dropped my head as uncertainty swamped me. I had no desire to leave my pack, but my mother may have been right. My mate might not be happy staying in the pack with me. Living in the same place with one of us miserable seemed the only way we could have a life together.

"What's got you so worked up?" Gates' sleepy grumble interrupted my swirling thoughts. I glanced up to see my mother gone, the door to my bedroom closed, and my mate smiling at me with heavy eyes.

I sighed and smiled at him. "Nothing. How are you feeling?"

Gates watched me for a long moment before closing his eyes and stretching.

"Tired, sore." He sniffed and lifted the sheet to look down his body. "And apparently dirty. I smell like blood and dirt."

"You kind of passed out when Shadow pulled out the bullet. We didn't want to do anything to wake you."

"Hmmmm, that makes sense." He sighed and closed his eyes again, wincing as he tried to lift his arm. "Damn it."

"What is it?"

"Nothing really. Just wishing I could return the favor to the fucker who took a chunk out of my arm." His eyes popped open. "Pardon my language."

I laughed and placed my hands on his chest. "No need to apologize. I've heard cussing before." I leaned over him and placed a small kiss to his dry lips. "I may have even said a few myself a time or two."

Gates wrapped his good arm around me and pulled me all the way down to lie on his chest. "Oh really, now? And what kinds of cussing are we talking about?"

"You want to know the words I've said?" I asked with a laugh.

"Yes, I do believe I need to know exactly how naughty your language can be, young Kaija, Omega of the Wariksen pack."

My smile faltered at the reminder of the possibility of losing my place in the pack, but I shook off the dread weighing me down and kissed my mate once more. Lightly, delicately. And then I slid my lips over his scruff-covered cheek to whisper in his ear.

"I have been known to say 'fuck' a time or two."

Gates growled and rolled, pulling me underneath him and pressing his hips into mine. He was hard...so hard all over. From the muscles in his arms to the planes of his chest to the erection that lay between us as he ran his nose up my neck.

"Say it again."

I dropped my head back as his teeth met my skin, a shiver working its way down my spine.

"Fuck."

My breathy whisper was met with the rolling of Gates' hips, his hard and hot pushing perfectly against my soft and wet. There was nothing between us but the belief we needed someone else's approval before we could progress to what we both wanted. And that belief was fading with every pass of the head of his dick over my clit.

I groaned and canted my hips as his tongue trailed along my throat. "Please."

Instead of my request bringing more from Gates, it resulted in his stopping the movement of his hips and pushing away from me.

"We can't." He swallowed hard. I stared at him, unsure of

why we had to stop.

"You're my mate. I want you, and my heat has passed. We can."

He huffed a laugh and sat back on his calves as he ran a hand through his hair. "Fuck, princess. I want you, too."

I sat up. His eyes fell to my naked breasts and he groaned.

"If you want me and I want you, why can't we be together?"

Gates yanked the sheet from around his legs and draped it over my shoulders.

"Because we've waited this long, and I want to do things right for once." He gave me a soft kiss, a simple press of his lips, before he jumped out of bed. "I'm going to take care of what business I need to. You"—he looked me over, lust and desire so plain in his eyes and the upward curve of his erection—"would probably feel better after a hot shower."

I pouted as he yanked his jeans over his hips and grabbed his shirt. "You could always join me, you know."

Gates chuckled as he settled the black fabric over his chest and reached for the leather vest he always wore, the one that identified him as a Feral Breed member. "I don't think I could keep my promise if I were to see you naked and wet. Again."

He winked at me as I blushed, remembering the night of my bath. That was less than forty-eight hours ago, and yet it felt as if a lifetime had passed.

Gates strode across the room to lean over me. His fingers grasped the edge of the sheet, pulling it down as he stared into my eyes.

"You are the most perfect thing I've ever seen in this very long life of mine." He rubbed his nose along my cheek, and then rested his forehead against mine as his eyes trailed down my body. "So beautiful and sweet. You deserve better than me, but the fates have given you to me as a gift, and I fully intend to treat you with all the love and respect I can offer. So let me do things the right way. I promise, it'll be worth your while."

I nodded once before pressing my lips to his one final time. "Then go, mate. Do what you need to, but be quick."

He pulled away, his eyes intense, before grinning and racing for the door. "I can be a lot of things for you, princess. Quick will never be one of them."

AN HOUR LATER, AFTER a long shower and a meal, I walked the camp toward where our funeral pyres were burning. The fire was a necessity—no humans could find our bodies. There would be too much danger of someone discovering the secret. Normally we burned one body at a time and mourned the loss to our pack. But as I approached the field where multiple fires raged, a sense of celebration was in the air.

Men danced with their mates, children ran around the edges of the field, catching fireflies and whooping with delight, and in the far corner, the Feral Breed boys stood in a group, laughing and talking with a few pack members.

I checked over the group, looking for Gates, but he was nowhere to be seen. The Breed all tended to dress the same— jeans, black boots, black leather vest with Breed logo on the back thrown over a dark T-shirt. All of them were attractive men, but none could compare to my mate. Who was definitely not among their group. He was near, though. I could feel him. I just couldn't see him.

I strolled through the field, smiling as my packmates greeted me. The evening was so surreal. I was being smiled at and hugged for participating in the deaths of other shifters. And though I knew in my head that their deaths were the only thing that saved me and my pack from further danger, my heart rejected the idea that they'd earned their fate. No one was irredeemable.

As I weaved through a group of human mates chatting near a low fire, my father whistled loudly from the far end of the field.

"I understand my daughter is well enough to join us in celebration of the defeat of our enemy."

I smiled as I came around the final fire. My father stood facing his pack, tall and regal as ever with his white hair and beard practically glowing in the dusky evening light. He met my gaze and gave me a wink before addressing the pack.

"Yesterday, the fates bestowed their graces upon us in battle, and we as a pack walked away hearty and whole. Those who were injured are healing, a true blessing from the gods. Tonight, as we release the bad energies from pack land, we shall celebrate one more blessing."

He turned to face west. I mimicked his position, staring into the trees still glowing with the setting sun. But then a shadow appeared, growing larger with every second, moving toward us.

"Welcome to our land," my father intoned, arms in the air. "We are the noble shifter brothers who came to these shores centuries ago. Our ancestors are the blessed white wolves of Finland, the honored protectors of ancient tribesmen who lived along the shores of the many lakes of our home country. We are family and friends, mates and neighbors. We are the Valkoisus pack."

I took a deep breath as excitement bloomed in my stomach. I knew those words. They were said every time a mate was brought into the pack. The seconds seemed to stretch on forever as my impatience to hear the next part of the speech grew. For the next few words would tell me whether the person coming was human or wolf. Whether the shadow in the woods was my Gates or someone else.

"Wolf brother—"

My heart exploded into a gallop. The shadow was a male shifter. This was it. My mate had finally come for me, and our Rites of Klunzad would begin within a few moments.

"—you have come to request one of our packsisters as your eternal mate."

My breaths came fast and hard as my head began to swim. I stretched onto my toes to see over the shoulder of the woman standing in front of me, but to no avail. The shadow remained a shadow.

"You have made your interest clear and shown your respect of our ancient ways. I welcome you onto Valkoisus pack land. Please come forward, offer yourself to your chosen mate, and let her choose her future."

The crowd parted as the shadow emerged from the tree line. Tall and strong, Gates strode across the field, the black cloak he wore fanning out around him. His eyes locked on mine as he drew closer, serious and intense. I could barely breathe, couldn't stop my body from shaking in anticipation of this moment.

I'd waited years to be joined with my fated mate. And right then, I knew the wait had been worth it. Because in the end, I would get Gates. And he was worth any wait the universe chose to throw my way.

When he reached the center of the circle formed by my packmates, Gates stopped and removed his hood. His gaze stayed locked on mine even as he began his part of the ceremony.

"My name is Lorenzo Martinez de Caballero, Gatekeeper of the Feral Breed. I offer blessings and thanks to the Valkoisus pack. I have come this evening with the approval of your Alpha to request a joining with my fated mate. Her spirit speaks to me, and her soul is entwined with mine. I offer myself to Kaija Wariksen, Omega of the Valkoisus pack, as mate, lover, and protector."

As was tradition, he kneeled and sat back on his heels. It

was my turn. I could refuse him; it was my right. But mate refusals among shifters were practically unheard of. And by the soft upturn of Gates' lips, he knew my decision before I began my way through the crowd toward him.

"You have chosen me, Lorenzo Martinez de Caballero?"

"Yes."

I smiled as I stopped directly in front of him. "You request my companionship, my love, and my attention?"

"Yes." He grinned back, his face level with my breasts.

I placed my hands on his shoulders. "You will fight for me and with me to protect our family, our pack, and our breed?"

"Yes." His hands gripped my hips and pulled me closer. I leaned over and licked my lips before placing them against his ear.

"You desire my flesh."

He shivered under my hands and gave me a throaty, "Yes."

I pulled away, meeting his gaze once more. "And will you join with me in the ways of a man and a woman? Will you mate with me? Will you complete our bond with the mating bite?"

Gates' eyes practically glowed with the fire of his lust. When he spoke his reply, his voice was strong and loud, without a hint of question.

"Hell yes."

I grinned. "Then I accept your request, sir."

He was off his knees and had me in his arms before I could breathe. His lips crashed into mine, tongues sliding together as we held each other tight. My legs wrapped around his hips, and his hands slid to cup my ass as I sank into his hold.

"Easy, kids." My father's voice interrupted our moment of rejoicing, and we broke apart, grinning.

"You are my mate now," I whispered as he placed his forehead against mine.

"I've been your mate from the first moment I saw you in

that cave. And I'll be your mate until my final breath." He squeezed my ass as he pulled me tighter against the erection trapped between us.

I clawed at his back and moaned. "Such a smooth talker."

"I do try." He grinned and kissed me again.

"And so we have a new mated pair!" My father's booming voice interrupted our moment again, and I laughed as Gates finally let me stand once more.

"Daughter mine, I wish you nothing but happiness in your mating. May you and Lorenzo be blessed with a union spanning centuries. Lorenzo"—he grasped Gates' hand and tugged him closer—"take care of my baby, or I will hunt you down and sell your pelt to the highest bidder."

The Feral Breed brothers laughed loudly. Even Gates himself had a bigger grin on his face.

"Yes, sir."

My father nodded then turned back to the pack around us.

"Come!" he exclaimed, throwing his hands in the air. "Let us escort these two to the blessed cabin so they can begin their Rites of Klunzad."

Every wolf in the field yipped in cheer, a cacophony of sound amplified by the roaring flames behind us. I stepped forward to hug my parents before returning to Gates' side. When I looked up, he was watching me, a heated look in his eyes. I blushed and grinned as Gates smirked. Everyone knew what the Rites cabin was—a place to safely complete your mating away from the distractions of the rest of the pack. It was private, secluded, and perfect for a few days getting to know someone you would be tied to for the rest of your life.

Gates pulled me into his arms, a final embrace before we made the two-mile trek to the cabin. "I promised I would come for you, and I am a man of my word."

I nuzzled deeper into his neck, my body responding to the

vibrations of his voice. His hand ran down my hair, sliding along the silky waves and pressing into my back. The touch was soothing, but my body craved more. More contact, more pressure, more skin. Both sides of me, human and wolf, were crazy to get our mate alone. To care for him, clean him, and check his wounds so we could help him heal. It was a desperate need, one that had me breathing hard and shivering as I fought against it.

He ran his nose along my jaw and behind my ear, scenting me, making my head drop back in the pleasure of his touch. I moaned, soft and long, as he dropped a kiss on my neck.

"Come." Gates pulled me along, following the flow of packmates as they escorted us to the cabin. "Let us start our bonding period."

Three days. We would have three days alone to complete our bond. As I clung to his hand and followed him toward the path leading farther into the north woods, I knew those three days would never be enough.

FIFTEEN

KAIJA'S PACK LED THE way to the Rites cabin, singing and laughing as they meandered down the wooded trail. In eras past, mating and claiming was done outdoors, the participants shifting from wolf and back multiple times over the course of three days. As cultures evolved, small structures were built to offer the newly mated couple privacy and protection from the elements.

I always found it a bit odd, the idea of building a house specifically for a newly mated couple to have sex in. Some Rites cabins were actually used for other reasons—small weddings, sometimes childbirth depending upon setup, time away when the pack dynamic grated on the human need for solitude.

But in the end, it was a structure built so couples like us could have sex without the rest of the pack listening in.

Odd indeed.

"It's right around the bend." Kaija glanced at me, the candlelight giving her a golden glow that nearly made me stumble. She was so stunningly beautiful. From her plump lips to her ample breasts, her big eyes to her rounded hips. A curvaceous, luscious example of everything a woman should be. And she was mine.

The wolf side of me agreed with the human perceptions, liking the way our mate moved, especially the sway of her hips. The needs of the wolf were much simpler than the man—eat, sleep, fuck, fight. Not necessarily in that order. And right now, with my mate so close I could smell her sweet scent, those instincts were focused on the fucking.

At the end of a sharp turn in the path, we came to a small clearing. A huge stone pillar rose straight above us, piercing the evening sky, and shading the entire area. The Rites cabin sat quiet in the lee of the rock, protected by the giant piece of stone.

The collection of rowdy shifters grew quiet as Kaija and I stepped onto the wood deck that served as a porch. I wrapped my arm around her shoulders and pulled her into my side.

"Thank you, Valkoisus pack, for welcoming me onto your land and allowing me the great honor of taking this beautiful, wonderful creature as my mate. I can never describe the joy I have found after four hundred long years without her." I looked over the crowd once more and grinned. "Now leave."

The pack laughed and offered us one more cheer before turning and going back the way they came. My Breed brothers stayed, though.

"That means you guys, too." I tried to look stern, but I was too happy to get much more than a grimace out before my smile took over once more.

"We're going." Sandman stepped forward with Pup at his side. "Shadow wanted to be here, but he's working with Doc Booth to help reset a few of Magnus' bones."

He turned his attention to Kaija. "We welcome you to the brotherhood of the Feral Breed, Kaija Wariksen. While you have not pledged our club or chosen to vie for membership, we have given you a road name for all you've done to save one of our most honored and respected club members. Be proud, be brave, and be feral…Princess of the Feral Breed."

Kaija grinned. She looked up at me with so much joy in her eyes, I couldn't resist. I crashed my lips to hers for a heated kiss before smacking her on the ass.

"Go ahead."

She rushed toward Sandman, jumping at him when she was near enough.

"Thank you so much." She hugged Sandman with abandon, and he took the affection in stride. But when she moved on to aggressively hold on to the younger Pup, he turned beet red and looked like he didn't know what to do with his arms.

"Easy there, Princess." I stepped off the porch, not wanting even the few feet between my mate and me. "I don't think Pup is used to such attention."

She smiled at me over her shoulder as Pup rolled his eyes.

"I get attention from females. I'm just not used to ones so…short."

I laughed as Kaija growled and wagged her finger at the shifter. "You'd better watch it, young one. I'm not afraid to turn you over my knee."

Sandman snorted. "He'd probably like that."

The group dissolved into laughter. We hadn't been able to relax and just be brothers for too long, not since Magnus had come aboard to run the club. It was a good feeling to once again laugh and joke with my brothers.

I didn't look forward to telling them I would not be returning to Detroit.

"Okay, okay. How about we let the lovebirds get on with their bonding?" Sandman gave Kaija one last hug before strolling my way. While my mate was distracted by the attention of saying goodbye to Pup, Sandman pulled me slightly to the side.

"We'll be on the north and east sides of the cabin—close,

but not too close. The Cleaners are stationed south and west, though we only have them for the night. Starting tomorrow, they will be pack wolves handpicked by Rex. No one will get near you, my brother."

I nodded and shook his hand. "Thank you."

"You would do the same for any one of us, and have guarded many a newly mated pair over the years, Gatekeeper. There are no thanks necessary."

I nodded, knowing he was right. Pup and Sandman soon said their goodbyes before heading off into the woods. I was alone...in the woods...with my mate. And I suddenly had no idea what to do next.

"We're finally alone." Kaija looked up at me with a soft smile on her face.

Shaking off my nervousness, I gripped her hand. "Come, my mate. Let me love you for a while."

I swung open the door to what would become the place of our first coupling. Entering the cabin before Kaija, I surveyed it for her safety before allowing her to follow me inside. It was exactly as I would have expected—clean and simple, with no walls to separate the living areas from the bedroom. A couch, two chairs, and a small table were all the furniture in the seating area, a round kitchen table on one end serving as the dining room. There was a small walled-off section at the back—the bathroom, I assumed.

But it was the bed that was the most impressive.

Massive was the only word to describe it. The headboard ran from the floor almost to the ceiling, an intricately carved wood sculpture to sleep under. Or not sleep. The mattress was bigger than any I'd ever seen—large enough to fit two or three couples easily. There was a footboard in the same style as the headboard, hand-carved with scenes of the mountains and forest that surrounded this land. The entire thing took up almost a third of the cabin, leaving very little room for the single nightstand and rocking chair in the sleeping area.

Kaija froze when she saw the bed, her eyes wide and her face slack. I understood her sudden fear. We had barely met, knew very little about each other, yet we were expected to use that bed for the next three days to satisfy our…needs. Sure, we'd been building up to what was to come with our time alone, but the sight of the bed put an extreme amount of pressure on the both of us.

This was one of the few times in my life when I realized just how fucked up being a shifter could be.

"How would you like me?" she whispered, her voice uneven. I sighed and ran a hand over my face. Four hundred years old and I felt like a virgin pup on his first go with a woman.

Instead of answering, I pulled her into my arms and rested my cheek upon the top of her head. She shivered in my hold but returned the embrace with a sigh on her lips. I ran my hands up and down her back, loving the way my fingers pressed into her flesh, the softness I encountered at every dip and swell. This was my mate, the woman who completed me, and I needed to make sure she was comfortable before I claimed her as such.

The scents of other wolves from the pack were on her skin and in her hair, ratcheting my anxiety higher. I needed her clean, I needed to make sure she was not injured from the day before, and I needed to get the blood of her captor off my body before I ripped my own skin off in a fit of jealous rage.

"Come," I said, holding out a hand. It took her a few seconds of internal debate, but finally she placed her hand in mine. I smiled at her, hoping she could see how much I wanted to take care of her, to make sure she was happy and healthy and whole.

"Where are we going?"

"It's time to take a shower."

Kaija

A SHOWER...MY MATE wanted to bathe with me.

I took a deep, shuddering breath. The night felt much more important than I had thought it would, the pressure of getting everything right immense. Instead of throwing me on the bed to have his way with me as I thought he would do, Gates wanted to wash me. I had no idea how to process that.

Once we were in the bathroom, he turned to me, those ice blue eyes tracking my face as if cataloguing my features. At the heated desire on his face, I relaxed. He made me feel beautiful with nothing but a look, made me feel vibrant and desired. There was no need to be nervous.

"Are you ready for this?" he asked, his voice more growl than ever. My whole body trembled, impatience and desire interwoven and leading my emotions. With no response needed, I pulled my scarlet cloak over my head. I was left in nothing but the lingerie I'd thrown on in haste before leaving for the burning—a simple set made of white lace with pink trim. There was nothing necessarily sexy about it, but the innocence of the colors spoke to my human side. He'd seen me bare more than once, had his tongue and fingers inside my body. Covering myself with the lacy, flimsy fabric had somehow seemed sexier than baring myself once again.

His eyes slid down my body, his approval obvious in the way his face flushed and his breathing increased. But when I pulled a bra strap over my shoulder, he stayed my hand.

"Wait."

I froze, anxiousness and the animal need his darkened look made me feel warring with each other. "Why?"

He shook his head and took a step closer. "You're so perfect for me. Strong and confident, yet still soft and sweet. You're everything I've ever dreamed of for a mate." He reached up and pulled his cloak over his head, standing before me in nothing but the faded denim he wore underneath. "You are this pristine, beautiful gift the fates have given me. And I intend to unwrap you properly."

With shaking hands, he slipped his fingers under the straps of my bra and drew them down my arms. The fabric fell, catching on the upper curve of my breast. Gates stared at where white fabric met my soft flesh, eyeing the darkened skin of my nipple peeking over the lace. He swallowed hard, and then brought his hand up to run his finger down the swell of my breast. My skin pebbled under his touch, the need within me growing hot and bright with every second that passed.

"So pretty."

His whispered confession calmed me in ways nothing else could have. It was honest and pure, something sweet in a moment filled with desire. He wrapped one hand around my waist and pulled me closer, pressing us together as he used a single hand to unhook my bra.

"You're good at that."

He smirked as he pulled the fabric down my arms and tossed it to the side. Once my breasts were fully bared to him, he took a moment to hold me before dropping to his knees. He slid the white panties down my thighs, letting them pool at my ankles.

"Up." He pulled on one ankle. I lifted my leg for him and he guided the fabric off my body, repeating the motion on the other side. And when he was done, when I stood naked and wanting before him, shivering with the restraint needed to keep from simply attacking him on the tile floor, he sighed.

"I will never deserve you."

"Try." My answer was automatic, something unstoppable and true. I hadn't meant it as a challenge. Still, his eyes darted to meet mine, shocked and uncertain. I gave him a small smile as he peered up at me, willing him to understand the meaning behind my answer. How much I believed in him, how desperately I wanted him to find his worth in our relationship. How I wanted us to be equals.

Finally, after several seconds of eye contact that might have been more intimate than any touch he could have offered, he sighed and rose to stand before me.

"I will."

I nodded my acceptance of his simple promise. No words were spoken as I unbuckled his belt and pulled the leather through the belt loops. His fly was next, the buttons sliding free with a single tug. I kept my eyes locked with his as I pushed the denim over his hips. There was nothing sexual about what I was doing. The way he watched me, the feel of his skin under my fingers, the trust to stand naked in front of a person who was practically a stranger—no, my care for him wasn't sexual. It was intimate, something beautiful and unique. Something only the two of us would only ever have together.

I sank to my knees before him. I was his and he was mine, and there was nothing I wouldn't do to make sure he knew that. But right then, he needed me to take care of him. To cleanse him and to allow him to cleanse me. To show him how much I wanted him in more ways than sexual ones. To give him a chance as a man.

I ran my hands down his bare legs, past his knees, and over his calves. His muscles clenched as my hands passed over them, the only sound in the room that of his harsh breaths. I helped him step out of his jeans, running my hands back up his legs as I rose before him.

"Bathe with me." My statement came out on a whisper of air, but there was no doubting my request. Gates grabbed my hand and led me into the shower where he turned on the taps and let the hot water flow over us.

We washed each other slowly, carefully, with great attention to detail. Every inch was mapped and memorized, every curve and dip explored. I washed the reminders of the past day from him. Mud and blood and everything else ran down his body to the drain as I scrubbed. Shoulders, chest, back, arms, legs—I cleansed him. Renewed him.

The wounds from the battle the day before had nearly healed, but it was the signs of past injuries that made me frown. The subtle shadow of bullet holes, lines that could only be caused by blades and claws, textures that weren't like what skin should be—the man was a walking road map of a long and violent life. The tattoos he wore softened the look of the scars, adding color and elegance to my roughened soldier. I spent extra time dancing my fingers across the lines and flourishes, reading the words, honoring the gentle-looking woman he'd chosen to etch into his skin.

He sighed as my hands slid from his waist around to his bottom; he shuddered as they came around the front to stroke his hardness. I didn't linger, knowing this was not the moment for such things. But I wanted to. Long and thick with a slight curve up, just the sight was enough to make my knees go weak.

And then it was my turn. Gates washed me well, running his hands all around my hips and thighs, bathing my feet and ankles with as much care as my breasts. But what made me shudder and groan, made my nipples harden and my body throb with desire, was the feeling of his fingers as they carefully washed and conditioned my hair. Gentle and slow, he pulled out every tangle, made sure every lock was clean and soft.

When he was done, when he'd rinsed the last of the conditioner out of my hair and simply held me by my shoulders, his eyes grew dark, his face serious.

"I was born in Spain late in the sixteenth century." His voice was barely above a whisper, soothing and calm with a hint more of an accent than I'd ever heard from him. "I have one brother, as you know. His real name is Bastian, but he is known as the Beast of the Feral Breed. We found our destiny with the Breed. It's a responsibility we both take seriously.

"I'm not a young wolf, Kaija, nor am I in any way innocent. I have fought and killed, though never indiscriminately. I don't believe in living with guilt for exacting the justice deserved." His eyes held mine as he lowered his voice, his accent growing thick, making the words have a rhythm to them. A sensual cadence pulling me under their spell.

"I have not always done the right thing, but I've always had the right intentions. I am the Gatekeeper for the Feral Breed, but I wield that power with care and not callousness. My hands are dirty, my world is sometimes dark and violent, but my conscience is clear." He took a deep, shaky breath. "And I know I can be a good mate for you."

I held his gaze as he stopped moving, his hands resting on my shoulders. There was so much heat in his eyes, so much desire. This man was passion incarnate, and yet he had an aura of nervousness around him. As if he believed I would refuse our mating even though I had joined him in the Rites cabin. As if he expected me to reject him.

With a shaking breath and an intense expression on his face, he said, "My name is Lorenzo Martinez de Caballero, and I have been waiting for you for a long time."

My heart broke for my mate. Handsome, strong, and ridiculously sexy, but he seemed lonely. Four hundred years was a long time to go without a mate. Most wolves were mated well before their centennial birthday. I couldn't even image him waiting for me, year after year, wondering if he'd somehow missed the opportunity to find his love.

"You found me, mate. It took time, but you found me. And I will never let you go."

Gates pulled me into his arms, shoulders shaking and chest heaving. I held him and stroked his bare skin to comfort and ensure him of my presence. There was no doubt left to be had, no question of our bonding. We were meant to be together, and it was time to join ourselves to each other. We had waited long enough for this moment. We had been patient. But there were no more rules to follow, no more pack to worry about. The rest of the night and the next few days were all about us and what we wanted to do. And right then, I wanted to wipe that last shadow of doubt right off his pretty face. It was time to complete our bonding…time to exchange our mating bites.

I reached behind Gates and turned off the taps. Stepping onto the tiled floor, I pulled his hand and dragged him behind me. He followed me into the bedchamber, both of us wet but neither caring enough to stop for a towel. Knowing he would give me the respect to make the decisions on our coupling, I crawled onto the bed as soon as I reached it. No pausing. No sign of second thoughts or weakness. I wanted Gates to give himself to me, and I would give myself to him in return.

"Kaija." He stood and stared as I lay back on the bed and gave him a smile.

"Lorenzo."

He shivered as I spoke his name, lengthening the middle syllable and ending on a whisper. But he didn't move. He simply stood at the side of the bed and watched me for several long seconds.

Until he fell.

SIXTEEN

Gates

MY MATE—MY BEAUTIFUL, sweet, kindhearted mate—lay naked and waiting for me on a bed so large, I doubted I could reach from one side to the other. She looked small and delicate, like a sexy, sinful doll waiting to be played with.

And I definitely wanted to play with her.

I didn't try to be sexy or suave. After everything I'd told her, I figured hiding any part of my nature was a wasted effort. She knew the good and the bad, the history and my hope for the future…and she accepted all of it. So I did exactly what I wanted to do.

I fell on the bed next to her and yanked her into my arms as I rolled.

"Gates."

Her giggle warmed my soul and made me smile. I stopped in the middle of the bed, holding most of my weight off her body with my arms as I fit my hips between her thighs.

"Princess."

Her growl had my already hard cock practically weeping. Her legs fell farther apart, opening to me in a way that was blatantly sexual. I rolled my hips against hers as I stared into her eyes, giving and taking in turn, working us into a rhythm that would lead us to what we both craved.

Her hands gripped my shoulders as I slid my cock against her opening, never pushing in, simply giving her the pressure she needed to tease her into arousal. With every pass, the heat of her flesh increased, the skin becoming slippery as she grew wetter and more swollen.

"Gates." Her whisper came out as a plea, as a request for something more than I was giving her. I responded by dropping my head to her chest and taking one of her peach-hued nipples between my teeth. I bit softly at first, increasing the pressure until she arched into me with a hiss, never stopping the rolling of my hips.

On the next bite, she gripped my hair and pulled my head back, her eyes intense and so very bright.

"What do you want, Princess?"

Without pause, with no fear or uncertainty, she answered, "Claim me, mate."

I growled and pulled my hips back before sliding one hand down her body to grasp my cock.

"Are you sure you're ready?"

She nodded and angled her hips, needy. With a deep, tongue-tangling kiss and a single hard thrust, I seated myself fully inside her. I had to go still to keep from coming immediately. Hot and wet and soft and holy-mother-of-fucking-all-things-holy tight. I needed a moment, just a second to hold back the tingling in my balls. I needed to calm the fuck down so I wouldn't come before I could give her what she needed.

"Fuck, Gates. Please."

Such a dirty word falling from those lips had me spinning in a haze of lust. I nodded and pulled my hips back then pushed forward once more, sliding in that slick cavern which had instantly become my favorite place to be. In and out, pulling and pushing, we worked together to stay connected. Our breaths turned to pants, our rumbles of pleasure to snarls and full growls as we each progressed toward the mating climax.

"Oh fuck." I hissed as her nails scraped down my back, knowing she'd drawn blood. Soon, I would bite her and pull the essence of her shifter into my body. Just the thought of the mating bites had my cock growing harder, my hips moving faster, and my mouth dropping words like fire.

"So hot. So soft. Fuck, baby. You feel so good wrapped around me. I want to stay buried inside you for a week, sweet girl. See all the ways I can make you come. Fuck, yeah…squeeze me again. Yes."

She growled and pulled me closer, her lips moving to my neck. I felt her fangs against my skin, felt the way her pussy fluttered and throbbed around my cock. She was ready.

I focused on my wolf spirit, allowing the instincts of mating and breeding to lengthen my canines. Kaija was a step ahead of me, licking and sucking where my neck met my shoulder to prepare a spot for the claiming mark. The thought of that scar, of her teeth marks permanently on display on my body, was enough to send me hurtling toward the edge of the cliff.

"Now, pretty girl. I'm going to come."

She sank her teeth into my neck and came, her pussy squeezing my cock like a vise. I threw my head back and roared as I followed her, my entire body seizing up with the force of my orgasm. And then I swung down and bit her shoulder, sinking my teeth into her flesh and pulling in her life's essence. What felt like another orgasm washed over me, causing my body to tense and freeze as the pleasure rippled along my spine. The thread between us, the mating bond we'd both felt since that day in the cave, grew hot and solid. I felt her pleasure as my own, a pulsing, heady thing between us. I felt the way she cared for me, the way she desired me. I felt everything.

Seconds or minutes passed as we lay together, connected in every way possible. Her teeth in my flesh and mine in hers had destroyed whatever sense of time I should have had. The feeling of being truly joined with her, mated to her, claimed by her, made small things like time unimportant in my world. All I needed, all I wanted, was what I had wrapped around my body.

As the claiming frenzy wore off and the mating thread went back to being a feeling rather than a physical entity, I released her shoulder from my jaws. I rolled to my side, pulling her with me. She kissed down my throat as I settled her next to me. I'd never felt so weary, so completely relaxed and calm. Wanting her safe and to feel her against me, I settled her against my chest and then nearly wrapped my body around hers.

"What are you doing?" She giggled but held me tight as I covered us with the quilt.

"Settling you into our den."

"Our den, huh? We're moving into the cabin?"

I tossed the quilt over our heads. "No, a blanket fort. I need a nap with my mate before I claim you again."

She snuggled into my hold with a chuckle. "I thought mates could only claim each other once?"

"Once?" I pressed my already hardening cock against her thigh and growled. "Once will never be enough, Princess."

Kaija

THE MORNING OF OUR final day in the cabin dawned overcast and gloomy, typical of a fall day in the Upper Peninsula. Snow would come soon. The thought made the gloom seem appropriate, for there was still the uncertainty of my future with Gates looming over me. Did I request we stay with my pack? Or did I give up everything I loved and hop on the back of Gates' bike to head off to parts unknown? Could I even leave my family behind, my packmates and friends? Could he ever find peace in the structure of a traditional pack instead of the freedom of his Feral Breed club?

As my mind spun off into the land of a thousand questions, Gates curled around me and pulled me close. As if he sensed my unrest. I settled against his chest, my head resting on his bicep as he fell deeper into sleep. This was it…our last day. Before nightfall, we would rejoin the pack, and I would announce to my family and pack what plans we'd made. If any.

I sighed as I watched my mate sleep, his face peaceful and his naked body warm against mine. Whatever we decided upon, he was mine. And I felt so lucky to have found him.

Wanting a break from my own thoughts—and knowing this was our last chance at privacy until we settled wherever we chose—I placed one hand on his hip and carefully pushed him over. He rolled to his back, one arm thrown over his head, the sheet we'd been tangled up in all night wrapped around the tops of his thighs.

His dick sat somewhat soft against his stomach. He'd been hard almost constantly since we'd arrived at the cabin, and I'd done my best to satisfy his needs. As he'd done his best to satisfy mine. We'd had sex in every position, every possible place within the cabin…and even once outdoors. My mate was a considerate lover and never left me wanting more.

And I wanted to be the same for him.

A craving for him washed over me, making me whimper. Who cared if we were on pack land or in a Breed den in Detroit—as long as we were together, we would find a way to be happy. And that was something to be celebrated.

I slid my body down the length of his, doing my best to keep from waking him. I'd been yanked from sleep in the middle of the night at one point by his mouth clamping over my clit and sucking. The sudden pleasure-pain of the moment led me to the fastest and strongest orgasm I'd ever experienced.

It was time to return the favor.

I settled against his side and leaned over to nuzzle the length of his dick. Gates didn't react, but his dick did. It lengthened and swelled as I continued to run my nose along him. When it was mostly hard, Gates groaned and slid his hand over his hipbone. Knowing my time for a sneak attack was quickly coming to a close, I leaned my upper body over his hips, grabbed his dick with one hand, and dropped my open mouth over the tip. I tightened my lips around his girth and quickly slid him all the way inside, sucking as I lifted back off.

Gates came awake with a jerk and a growl. He grabbed my head and thrust his hips up, forcing himself deeper. It was such a primal response, so much more raw than anything he'd done up to that point. While our coupling hadn't been gentle, he'd never just given in and done what he wanted to me without focusing on my pleasure first. But this time, it was all about him. And he took full advantage of that fact.

"Fuck, yes."

I returned his growl and let him fuck my mouth, drawing him as deep as I could before hollowing out my cheeks as he pulled out.

"Oh gods. Oh gods. Kaija…Princess…what…?"

I growled louder and bobbed my head faster, adding a hand to the base of his dick to keep him steady. He writhed and panted, cursing and growling as I worked him hard. When his legs spread and he groaned with what I knew was an impending orgasm, I grasped his balls in my hand and rolled them, giving him small tugs every few strokes.

"Baby…baby…I'm going…fuck, Kaija. So hot. Oh. Just a little…yes. Yes."

Gates nearly bowed off the bed, a roar rumbling out of him as he came. When he was done, when he fell back on the mattress after I'd suckled him until he'd once again gone soft, he shivered and pulled me up the length of him.

"What the hell was that?"

I smiled as he pushed a lock of hair out of my face. "Your wake-up call."

He chuckled and ran his hands up and down my back. Over my bottom. Around my hips.

"Can I get woken up like that more often?"

"Only if you're good."

He grinned and pulled me up to the head of the bed. He manipulated my body—the two of us laughing as we twisted and tumbled on the mattress—until I was on my knees, leaning forward to grip the headboard. And then he slid underneath me, peering up at me from where his head rested between my legs.

"I'm always good," he said right before he sucked my clit between his lips.

SEVENTEEN

Kaija

"FERAL BREED BROTHERS." MY mother stood on the porch with a small smile on her face. "You have lived up to the myth we pack wolves have heard since our youngest days. There is no way we can repay you for your assistance with rescuing our beloved packmates."

"There is no repayment needed." Shadow stepped toward the porch, his chin up and his cut sitting perfectly across his shoulders. "We're happy to have been of service to your most honorable pack. Should there be anything else we can do for you, please know you only have to contact us."

My mother nodded and stepped next to my father, who stood regal and stoic at the head of the crowd. Gates fisted the back of my cloak, which was the only outward sign of the tension he was shouldering within himself.

That man is not meant for pack life.

My mother's words played in my mind, bringing a heaviness to my heart that I couldn't explain. This was my pack, my home, and I didn't want to leave. But the men now swinging legs over leather seats were Gates' family, and they were about to ride away.

The one known as Magnus, who was still limping and looking a little more damaged than when he'd arrived, stared right at Gates as he mounted his motorcycle.

"You know you'll always be a Breed brother, Gatekeeper."

Gates' fist against my back shook as he answered. "We'll let you know once our plans are decided upon."

Magnus nodded as he started his bike. A mechanical thunder filled the air, nearly shaking the earth as the others followed suit. Only one didn't start his engine. He wasn't even sitting on his seat. Sandman stood with a hip resting against his bike and his arms crossed over his chest.

"Are you sure about this?"

Sandman glared at Gates, and an aggressive tension seemed to grow between the two. Rex moved up to stand on Gates' right; I was already on his left. My father and mother stepped off the porch to stand behind us. We were surrounding our newest packmate, giving him all the strength and support we could. Sandman must have recognized the maneuver, because he glanced at me with a snarl on his lips.

Gates growled and edged himself in front of me. "I'm sure."

Sandman looked away for a moment before striding to where we stood. He didn't acknowledge my warning growl or the way Rex glared daggers at him. Instead, he moved close enough to nearly touch Gates and spoke to him in a low whisper.

"And when her father is no longer Alpha? What then? If one of her brothers isn't strong enough to earn the seat, you know what could happen. There are no less than five wolves here who would give their eyeteeth to have your mate in their bed. If one of them or someone from their clan takes over, what's your backup plan?"

"I'll kill them myself."

"Funny thing. That's what I thought as well. It didn't work

out too well for me, did it?"

Gates growled long and low, a warning to the shifter before us.

"I won't try to start a coup against the Alpha like you did, son. If the time comes, I'll challenge him directly. As wolves should do."

The other Breed members turned off their bikes, leaving us in a heavy silence as the two men glared at each other.

"Is that what you believe?" Sandman edged closer, nearly rubbing shoulders with Gates. "You believe the bullshit story the packs tell to keep their members in line?"

"That's what happened."

"You don't know shit!" Sandman snarled and stepped back, gripping his hair in his hands as he paced. "I didn't challenge the Alpha of my pack. He called Alpha Prerogative on my Margaret, and she didn't want to bed him. When he came for her and she refused him, he tried to physically take her from our home."

Sandman huffed and grew quiet, his face falling with a sudden sadness that seemed too heavy for one man to carry.

"She didn't want him, and I didn't want to share her, so I fought. For three days, we battled while my so-called pack watched. And when it was over, when I had beaten him and limped home to find my mate, she was dead. The Alpha's chosen shewolf didn't like the attention Margaret was getting, so she killed her while I was too distracted to do anything about it."

He glanced at me, a lifetime of regret in his eyes.

"Alpha Prerogative, sneaky fuckers, jealous shewolves, forced Omega breedings, the threat from outside with this collector—you have it coming at you from all sides, yet you refuse to stay with your brothers who would kill for you. And for her. Without pause or doubt."

Gates didn't respond at first; he stood and watched Sandman

for a long moment. And when he did speak, his words didn't carry the confidence I was used to hearing from him.

"You lie."

"Do I? Call Blaze right now! He was there. He watched from the sidelines as I fought for my mate, not knowing what the shewolf was planning. He knows everything that happened. That's why he instituted new regulations within the NALB. He saw my pack fuck me in the worst possible way, and he promised to do his best never to allow it to happen again." He pointed over my shoulder as he once again charged at Gates. "You think Chinoo over there wouldn't call Alpha Prerogative the second he claimed the title? You think he's not dreaming of getting between Kaija's legs even now? You think the bastard who contracted the kidnapping in the first place won't come back for her? This pack, while strong, is not capable of fending off a large attack, and it's not the safest place for you or your new mate."

When Gates didn't respond, Sandman huffed and turned to walk away. "You can live in ignorant bliss until a new Alpha is determined or those assholes come back. That's your choice, oh mighty Gatekeeper. Whichever comes first, you'll lose Kaija at that point. And you fucking know it."

Gates roared and jumped, shifting in midair. His cloak fell to the ground as his wolf rushed forward. Sandman shifted as well, rolling as he was hit by the blur of black fur and flesh. I gasped and moved to step forward, but Rex immediately grabbed me and held me back. I screamed for Gates to stop as he ripped into his denmate, a man he saw as one of his brothers. A man he would most likely kill because of harsh words spoken in regards to my safety.

Teeth and claws and blood—for too many long minutes, that was all I knew. Sandman appeared to be avoiding the fight, instead focusing on defending himself from Gates' attack.

Taking hit after hit from the larger wolf. It had to end. Gates would never forgive himself if he hurt or killed one of his brothers. I struggled in my brother's hold but to no avail. He would not release me, and he would not listen to my pleas to stop the fight.

The other pack shifters inched forward, watching with interest. Their fascination sickened me. I wanted to scream at them to back off. To stop watching. To walk away. But I knew it would be of no use, for a fight among packmates was an opportunity to size up your competition.

My stomach sank as I finally understood how true Sandman's words were.

If my family didn't stay in power with the pack, the age-old custom of Alpha Prerogative could be reinstated. The Wariksen clan agreed it was a barbaric practice, taking away the woman's right to choose her partner and forcing her to breed with the unmated Alpha male. The very thought disgusted me, but the more traditional clans like the Donatis condoned the behavior as a way to strengthen pack bloodlines and bond clans. If one of them were to become Alpha, they could force Gates and me to comply with the order or face banishment. Or death.

I watched as the men around me studied the fighting wolves, all of them intense in their attention. Except one—Chinoo stood to the side by his father, the Elder Donati. While Chinoo practically leered at me, he whispered to his father, who was watching Gates with something akin to excitement in his eyes. The two made my skin crawl. But for the first time, I noticed how large Chinoo had become. Muscular and tall, he was probably one of the largest in the pack besides the men in my family. He would be a strong contender for Alpha when the time came. Bernte had already made his reluctance to the seat known, Rex's knee injury could be a hindrance if anyone challenged him, which left only Dante to fight for the Wariksen clan.

My heart raced and my stomach dropped. My mother's words kept repeating in my head, alternating with what Sandman had said.

The Feral Breed is more than a motorcycle club. It's a brotherhood.

You refuse to stay with your brothers who would kill for you.

There is no adjusting for men like him.

Whichever comes first, you'll lose Kaija at that point. And you fucking know it.

Life with a partner is not easy. There are sacrifices and compromises that must be made, on both sides, even with fate helping you along the way.

As Gates slammed into the side of Sandman and knocked him to the ground, I turned in Rex's arms.

"Release me."

"Kaija, you can't—"

"He's my mate, he needs me, and I am telling you to release me. Now."

Rex stared at me for a long moment before he dropped his arms from around me. "Don't do anything stupid, sister."

"I won't. But it's time for me to go." I gave him a small smile as his eyes grew wide.

Without another word, I stepped between the two fighting wolves, no longer afraid or undecided. My mate stopped and stared at me as his blood ran across his face from a gash over his eye.

"That's enough, Gatekeeper."

Gates growled, his eyes going to the fallen wolf behind me.

"It's enough. You've made your point well." I swallowed and took one last look at my pack. Men and women I'd known my entire life, others who had become packsisters and brothers as their fated mates had found them. All happy and healthy.

I couldn't bring danger back to their doorsteps. I couldn't knowingly put my nephews at risk when there were other options for me. My mother had said life with a mate would mean sacrifices. And I was finally ready to make one.

"I absolve my loyalty to the Valkoisus pack."

Gasps sounded through the crowd. Rex wrapped his arms around a surprised Lanie who stared at me with her mouth fallen open. My mother's eyes filled with tears, but she didn't look surprised. She and my father stood at the front of the group, dignified and strong…and looking prouder than I'd ever seen them.

"Are you sure of this, daughter?" my father asked. "Are you really choosing to leave our pack?"

I glanced at my mate. Even in his wolf form, I could see the shock he felt at my statement. This was not what we'd planned, but deep down, I knew it was the right decision.

"I'm sure. I choose to leave the pack and follow the Feral Breed with my mate."

Chinoo snorted. "Bitches can't join the Breed."

"Technically, that's not true." Shadow walked over, offering a pair of jeans to Sandman as he shifted into his human form. "There's never been a shewolf in the Breed, but there's nothing barring them from joining."

While Chinoo and Shadow argued Feral Breed regulations, Gates shifted to his human form, quickly donning his discarded cloak.

"You don't have to do this."

I lifted my chin and looked him in the eye. "I've made my decision, mate."

He clenched his jaw. "I won't bring you into the Feral Breed world. It's too dark for you. There's too much death and fighting for someone as sweet as you."

I stepped into the circle of his arms, running my hands up

his biceps. "I won't stay here and watch your wariness grow and poison our relationship. And I won't leave here as a nomad. You'll never be happy in a pack, and I'll never be happy without one."

"But the Breed isn't a pack."

"Yes, you are. Whether you realize it or not, your brotherhood, your bonds, are the purest form of pack I've ever seen. My pack would fight for me; yours would die for you." I lifted up onto the balls of my feet and pressed my lips to his. "Let me join you, Gatekeeper."

He growled low, his eyes dark and hungry. "You'd have to ride on the back of my bike out of here. We didn't bring the war wagon."

"Then I guess I should wear warm clothes." I bit his lip and released a soft rumble.

He gripped my hips and pulled me against him. "And if you miss your pack?"

"We'll visit."

He dropped his forehead to rest on mine and lowered his voice. "And if I'm not strong enough to protect you?"

I ran my fingers over his cheeks and jaw. "You will be as long as you have me with you. But if we need help, we'll call on our brothers."

He opened his mouth to speak but I placed my fingers over his lips to silence him.

"You are a member of the Feral Breed, a proud protector of the shifter community. It's a part of who you are, and nothing will ever change that. Would you deny me the opportunity to learn more about your life and the job you've chosen to do?"

"No, but—"

"No buts. Fate may have chosen you for me, but I choose the path leading me there. Don't belittle my decision by denying me what I've asked for."

He swallowed hard and rocked me from side to side. "I just want you safe and happy."

"And that's all I want for you. Staying here won't make either one of us happy, that much I know for sure. We need to go someplace else, someplace we can build a den together surrounded by friends and the people we choose to call pack."

I grinned, excitement making me want to yip and yell. This was it...our adventure was beginning, our life moving forward. The two of us would forge our own path, create our own pack bonds with the people we chose to have around us.

"So then we leave." The corners of Gates' lips inched up, his face brightening.

"So then we leave. Together."

"Together." Gates kissed me hard, full of passion and joy, before turning his attention to Sandman. "Thank you for beating some sense into me."

Sandman gave him a wry grin. "Hey, man. Someone had to do it. That ancient noggin of yours just wasn't picking up the hints."

Laughter pulsed from the shifters surrounding us, lightening the mood and turning my goodbye from a moment of surprise to a moment of celebration. I wrapped my arm around my mate's hips and smiled at my family and friends. I would come back to visit them, of that I was certain. But for the foreseeable future, I needed to support my mate in the work he'd chosen. There would be no pack fighting or Alpha challenges for us. We would find our fate on the highways. Together.

And if the leaders of the Feral Breed didn't like it, they could kiss my Princess tail.

A young shifter trying to find his place.

A witch searching for a place in her coven.

A love that breaks every boundary.

CLAIMING HIS WITCH

FERAL BREED MOTORCYCLE CLUB
BOOK THREE

AVAILABLE NOW

ACKNOWLEDGMENTS

To Esher, who continues to make me giggle on an almost daily basis. I may even come to Iowa one day just to say hi in person. Maybe.

To Heather, because she's my soul mate. Period.

To Lisa, for always making editing fun. Mostly. At least I know there will always be wine.

To my friend Madonna, who makes the world beautiful by just being in it.

And as always, to my husband, who deals with me and my crazy ideas much better than most would. Thank you for letting me take over the end of the dining room table so I could realize this dream.

Edited by Silently Correcting Your Grammar, LLC
Cover Art by Cormar Covers

ABOUT THE AUTHOR

A storyteller from the time she could talk, Ellis grew up among family legends of hauntings, psychics, and love spanning decades. Those stories didn't always have the happiest of endings, so they inspired her to write about real life, real love, and the difficulties therein. From farmers to werewolves, store clerks to witches—if there's love to be found, she'll write about it. Ellis lives in the Chicago area with her husband, daughters, and a giant dog who hogs the bed.

Find Ellis online at:
Website: www.ellisleigh.com
Twitter: https://twitter.com/ellis_writes
Facebook: https://www.facebook.com/ellisleighwrites

CPSIA information can be obtained at www.ICGtesting.com
Printed in the USA
LVOW11s1428050916

503273LV00001B/39/P